Last of the Curlews

FRED BODSWORTH

Last of
the Curlews

Illustrated by T. M. Shortt

The
Edwin Way Teale
Library of
Nature Classics

DODD, MEAD & COMPANY • NEW YORK

1 2 3 4 5 6 7 8 9 10

Library of Congress Cataloging-in-Publication Data
Bodsworth, Fred, 1918–
Last of the curlews.
1. Eskimo curlew. I. Title.
QL696.C48B63   1987   598'.33   87-24319
ISBN 0-396-09186-5
ISBN 0-396-09187-3 {PBK}

"The beauty and genius of a work of art may be re-conceived, though its first material expression be destroyed; a vanished harmony may yet again inspire the composer; but when the last individual of a race of living beings breathes no more, another heaven and another earth must pass before such a one can be again."

From THE BIRD: ITS FORM
      AND FUNCTION, by C. WILLIAM BEEBE

F O R E W O R D

Effective communication about environmental prob-
lems has taken many paths during the past several decades.
Studies published in scientific journals have reached the
scientific community, but seldom the general public. The
insidious effects of DDT and other pesticides on bird and
other animal populations really had little impact on the
public until Rachael Carson analyzed and summarized the
situation in a dynamic and popular work, SILENT SPRING,
in 1962.

Even before Earth Day in 1970, though, there were hundreds of thousands of people in this country and elsewhere who were becoming sensitive to and knowledgeable about the increasing degradation of the natural world. These people were nature enthusiasts, bird watchers, wildflower photographers and even a few "little old ladies in tennis shoes." They were members of the National Audubon Society, the Nature Conservancy, the Sierra Club.

Their interest in nature was largely spawned by a new invention: a series of pocket field guides with a new system of identifying natural objects created by Roger Tory Peterson. These books enabled every amateur to become expert on bird and plant identification. People became hooked on natural history and they began to have an increasingly vigorous and effective voice in shaping the environmental ethic of their neighbors and ultimately the country. Along the way a few naturalists were trying to express in a more gentle, yet effective, fashion their outrage at what was happening to nature. The new technique was fiction.

In this genre, Fred Bodsworth's LAST OF THE CURLEWS stands out as an effective means of communicating an environmental disaster: the extinction of an entire species.

One may argue that reaching inside the mind of any wild creature in order to relate its capability of reasoning, much less its emotional state, is over-reaching, unjustified and certainly unscientific, even as part of a legitimate effort to dramatize a real environmental issue. Perhaps. But Bodsworth's exceptional knowledge of the species he writes about, combined with his imaginary and anthropomorphic musings, build a logical storyline which may be legitimate in this instance. After all, it is a matter of judgement as well as passion when an author sets out to convince others of a real problem.

The main character of this novel, the Eskimo Curlew, is close to extinction when the tale begins. In fact as recently as the early 1950's when Bodsworth's work was being crafted, most ornithologists had given the bird up for lost. The demise of such a magnificent species, undoubtedly due to human activities, stimulated the author's story-telling when he discovered that an American soldier, an avid birder, had definitely identified two of the birds, possibly a mated pair, on a Galveston Island beach.

Interestingly, though, since that sighting in 1945 others have been spotted and positively identified in other parts of their range. In his EASTERN FIELD GUIDE TO THE BIRDS published in 1980, Roger Tory Peterson states that the Eskimo Curlew "Migrated along East Coast in fall, through Great Plains in spring. Recent sight records in several states."

Whatever the true current status of this species, Bodsworth treats it as if the population *had* disappeared, except for two individuals, a pair that meet only by chance after the male has spent a summer of wishful waiting for a mate on its tundra breeding grounds. The author expresses the male bird's forlorn feelings as it chases away female contenders of similar species for its attention. Finally the urge to migrate southward is overwhelming and the last male curlew joins a flock of shorebird migrants on a long journey. By chance but inevitably, the male finds the last female of its species. Readers' hopes soar: perhaps, just perhaps, the species will be saved.

Indeed, the loss of an entire species is a great tragedy, and maybe even this fictionalized account may move human behavior only slightly toward greater protection of the natural world. In any case, Bodsworth's well-told story should make each of us consider our role in a world with other species, species less durable than we.

Dr. Harold D. Mahan
President
Roger Tory Peterson Institute
Jamestown, New York

Last of the Curlews

CHAPTER ONE

By June the Arctic night has dwindled to a brief interval of grey dusk and throughout the long days mosquitoes swarm up like clouds of smoke from the potholes of the thawing tundra. It was then that the Eskimos once waited for the soft, tremulous, far-carrying chatter of the Eskimo curlew flocks and the promise of tender flesh that chatter brought to the arctic land. But the great flocks no longer come. Even the memory of them is gone and only the legends remain. For the Eskimo curlew, originally one of the continent's most abundant game birds, flew a gantlet of shot each spring and fall, and, flying it, learned too slowly the fear of the hunter's gun that was the essential of survival. Now the species lingers on precariously at extinction's lip.

The odd survivor still flies the long and perilous migration from the wintering grounds of Argentine's Patagonia, to seek a mate of its kind on the sodden tundra plains which slope to the Arctic sea. But the Arctic is vast. Usually they seek in vain. The last of a dying race, they now fly alone.

As the Arctic half-night dissolved suddenly in the pink and then the glaring yellow of the onrushing June day, the Eskimo curlew recognized at last the familiar S-twist of the ice-hemmed river half a mile below. In the five hundred miles of flat and featureless tundra he had flown over that night, there had been many rivers with many twists identical to this one, yet the curlew knew that now he was home. He was tired. The brown barbs of his wing feathers were frayed and ragged from the migration flight that had started in easy stages below the tropics and had ended now in a frantic, non-stop dash across the treeless barren grounds as the full frenzy of the mating madness gripped him.

The curlew set his wings and dropped stone-like in a series of zigzagging side-slips. The rosy-pink reflections of ice pans on the brown river rushed up towards him. Then he leveled off into a long glide that brought him to earth on the oozy shore of a snow-water puddle well back from the river bank.

Here for millenniums the Eskimo curlew males had come with the Junetime spring to claim their individual nesting plots. Here on the stark Arctic tundra they waited feverishly for the females to come seeking their mates of the year. As they waited, each male vented the febrile passion of the breeding time by fighting savagely with neighboring males in defense of the territory he had chosen. In the ecstasy of home-coming, the curlew now hardly remembered that for three summers past he had been mysteriously alone and the mating fire within him had burned itself out unquenched each time as the lonely weeks passed and, inexplicably, no female had come.

The curlew's instinct-dominated brain didn't know or didn't ask why.

He had been flying ten hours without stop but now his body craved food more than rest, for the rapid heartbeat and metabolism that had kept his powerful wing muscles flexing rhythmically hour after hour had taken a heavy toll of body fuel. He began probing into the mud with his long bill. It was a strange bill, curiously adapted for this manner of feeding, two-and-a-half inches long, strikingly down-curved, almost sickle-like. At each probe the curlew opened his bill slightly and moved the sensitive tip in tiny circular motions through the mud as he felt for the soft-bodied larvae of water insects and crustaceans. The bill jabbed in and out of the ooze with a rapid sewing-machine action.

There were still dirty grey snowdrifts in the tundra hollows but the sun was hot and the flat Arctic world already

teemed with life. Feeding was good, and the curlew fed without stopping for over an hour until his distended crop at the base of his throat bulged grotesquely. Then he dozed fitfully in a half-sleep, standing on one leg, the other leg folded up close to his belly, his neck twisted so that the bill was tucked deeply into the feathers of his back. It was rest, but it wasn't sleep, for the curlew's ears and his one outside eye maintained an unrelaxing vigil for Arctic foxes or the phantom-like approach of a snowy owl. His body processes were rapid and in half an hour the energy loss of his ten-hour flight was replenished. He was fully rested.

The Arctic summer would be short and there would be much to do when the female came. The curlew flew to a rocky ridge that rose about three feet above the surrounding tundra, alighted and looked about him. It was a harsh, bare land to have flown nine thousand miles to reach. Its harshness lay in its emptiness, for above all else it was an empty land. The trees which survived the gales and cold of the long winters were creeping deformities of birch and willow which, after decades of snail-paced growth, had struggled no more than a foot or two high. The timberline where the trees of the sub-arctic spruce forests petered out and the tundra Barren Grounds began was five hundred miles south. It was mostly a flat and undrained land laced with muskeg ponds so close-packed that now, with the spring, it was half hidden by water. The low gravel humps and rock ridges which kept the potholes of water from merging into a vast, shallow sea were covered with dense mats of grey reindeer moss and lichen, now rapidly turning to green. A few inches below lay frost as rigid as battleship steel, the land's foundation that never melted.

The curlew took off, climbed slowly, and methodically circled and re-circled the two-acre patchwork of water and moss that he intended to claim as his exclusive territory. Occasionally, sailing slowly on set, motionless wings, he would utter the soft, rolling whistle of his mating song. There was nothing of joy in the song. It was a warcry, a warning to all who could hear that the territory had an owner now, an owner flushed with the heat of the mating time who would defend it unflinchingly for the female that would come.

The curlew knew every rock, gravel bar, puddle and bush of his territory, despite the fact that in its harsh emptiness there wasn't a thing that stood out sufficiently to be called a landmark. The territory's western and northern boundaries were the top of the river's S-twist which the curlew had spotted from the air. There was nothing of prominence to mark the other boundaries, only a few scattered granite boulders which sparkled with specks of pyrite and mica, a half dozen birch and willow shrubs and a few twisting necks of brown water. But the curlew knew within a few feet where his territory ended. Well in towards the centre was a low ridge of cobblestone so well drained and dry that, in the ten thousand years since the ice age glaciers had passed, the mosses and lichens had never been able to establish themselves. At the foot of this parched stony bar where drainage water from above collected, the moss and lichen mat was thick and luxuriant. Here the female would

select her nesting site. In the top of a moss hummock she would fashion out a shallow, saucer-like depression, line it haphazardly with a few crisp leaves and grasses and lay her four olive-brown eggs.

The curlew circled higher and higher, his mating song becoming sharper and more frequent. Suddenly the phrases of the song were tumbled together into a loud, excited, whistling rattle. Far upriver, a brown speck against the mottled grey and blue sky, another bird was winging northward, and the curlew had recognized it already as another curlew.

He waited within the borders of his territory, flying in tightening circles and calling excitedly as the other bird came nearer. The female was coming. The three empty summers that the male had waited vainly and alone on his breeding territory were a vague, tormenting memory, now almost lost in a brain so keenly keyed to instinctive responses that there was little capacity for conscious thought or memory. Instinct took full control now as the curlew spiraled high into the air in his courtship flight, his wings fluttering moth-like instead of sweeping the air with the deep strokes of normal flight. At the zenith of the spiral his wings closed and the bird plunged earthwards in a whistling dive, leveled off a few feet above the tundra and spiraled upwards again.

The other bird heard the male's frenzied calling, changed flight direction and came swiftly toward him. But instinctively obeying the territorial law that all birds recognize, she came to earth and perched on a moss-crowned boulder well outside the male's territory.

The male was seething now with passion and excite-

ment. He performed several more courtship flights in rapid
succession, spiraling noisily upward each time until almost
out of sight, then plunging earthward in a dive that barely
missed the ground. for several minutes the female nonchalantly preened her wing feathers, oblivious to the love
display. Then, alternately flying and running across the tundra
a few quick wing beats or steps at a time, she moved into
the mating territory and crouched submissively, close to
where the male was performing.

1 0

The male whistled shrilly and zoomed up in a final nuptial flight, hovered in mid-air high above the crouching female, then dropped like a falling meteorite to a spot about six feet from where she waited. He stood for a moment, feathers fluffed out and neck out-stretched, then walked stiff-legged toward her.

When still a yard away, the male abruptly stopped. The whispering courtship twitter that had been coming from deep in his throat suddenly silenced, and a quick series of alarm notes came instead. The female's behavior also suddenly changed. No longer meekly submissive, she was on her feet and stepping quickly away.

The male abandoned his courtship stance, lowered his head like a fighting cock and dashed at the female. She dodged sideways, and took wing. The male flew in pursuit, calling noisily and striking repeatedly at her retreating back.

The curlew's mating passion had suddenly turned into an aggressive call to battle. The female was a trespasser on his territory, not a prospective mate, for at close range he had recognized the darker plumage and eccentric posture of a species other than his own. The other bird was a female of the closely related Hudsonian species, but the Eskimo curlew knew only, through the instinctive intuition set up by nature to prevent infertile matings between different species, that this bird was not the mate he awaited.

He chased her a quarter of a mile with a fury as passionate as his love had been a few seconds before. Then he returned to the territory and resumed the wait for the female of his own kind that must soon come.

Two curlew species, among the longest legged and

longest billed in the big shorebird family of snipes, sandpipers and plovers to which they belong, nest on the Arctic
tundra—the Eskimo curlew and the commoner and slightly
larger Hudsonian. Though distinct species, they are almost
indistinguishable in appearance.

The Arctic day was long, and despite the tundra gales
which whistled endlessly across the unobstructed land the
day was hot and humid. The curlew alternately probed the
mudflats for food and patrolled his territory, and all the time
he watched the land's flat horizons with eyes that never relaxed. Near mid-day a rough-legged hawk appeared far to
the north, methodically circling back and forth across the

river and diving earthward now and then on a lemming that incautiously showed itself among the reindeer moss. The curlew eyed the hawk apprehensively as the big hunter's circling brought it slowly upriver towards the curlew's territory. Finally the rough-leg crossed the territory boundary unmarked on the ground but sharply defined in the curlew's brain. The curlew took off in rapid pursuit, his long wings stroking the air deeply and his larynx shrieking a sharp piping alarm as he closed in on the intruder with a body weight ten times his own. For a few seconds the hawk ignored the threatened attack, then turned back northward without an attempt at battle. It could have killed the curlew with one grasp of its talons, but it was a killer only when it needed food, and it gave ground willingly before a bird so maddened with the fire of the mating time.

The sun dipped low, barely passing from view, and the curlew's first Arctic night dropped like a grey mist around him. The tundra cooled quickly, and as it cooled the gale that had howled all day suddenly died. Dusk, but not darkness, followed.

The curlew was drawn by an instinctive urge he felt but didn't understand to the dry ridge of cobblestone with the thick mat of reindeer moss at its base where the nest would be. In his fifth summer now, he had never seen a nest or even a female of his kind except the nest and mother he had briefly known in his own nestling stage, yet the know-how of courtship and nesting was there, unlearned, like a carry-over from another life he had lived. And he dozed now on one leg, bill tucked under the feathers of his back,

beside the gravel bar which awaited the nest that the bird's instinct said there had to be.

Tomorrow or the next day the female would come, for the brief annual cycle of life in the Arctic left time for no delays.

PHILOSOPHICAL
TRANSACTIONS
of THE ROYAL SOCIETY
of LONDON
giving some ACCOUNT of the present
undertakings, studies and labours
of the
INGENIOUS
in many considerable parts of the world.
Vol. LXII for the year 1772.

Article xxix.

An account of the birds sent from Hudson's Bay; with observations relative to their natural history; and Latin descriptions of some of the most uncommon. By Mr. J. Reinhold Forster, F.R.S.

From the factory at Hudson's Bay, The Royal Society were favoured with a large collection of uncommon quadrupeds, birds, fishes, &C., together with some account of their names, place of abode, manner of life, uses, by Mr. Graham, a gentleman belonging to the settlement on Severn River; and the governors of the Hudson's Bay Company have most obligingly sent orders, that these communications should be from time to time continued.

(The birds described by Mr. Forster being all introduced into Mr. Latham's ornithological volumes, under the same titles, it becomes unnecessary to give the Latin descriptions, which are therefore omitted from these transactions.)

1. Falco columbarius. Pigeon hawk. It is migratory. 2. . . . . 3. . . . . 4. . . . .

18. New species. Scolopax borealis. Eskimaux curlew. This species of curlew, is not yet known to the ornithologists; the first mention made of it is in The Faunula Americae Septentrionalis, or Catalogue of North American Animals. It is called wee-kee-me-nase-su, by the natives; feeds on swamps, worms, grubs, &C., visits Albany Fort in April or

beginning of May; breeds to the northward, re-
turns in August, and goes away southward again
the latter end of September in enormous flocks.

CHAPTER TWO

The hot days and chilling nights raced by, the snowdrifts disappeared even from the shaded hollows, the austere browns and greys of the tundra became a flaming carpet of pink and yellow blooms, and the female curlew never came. Other shorebirds came in their hundreds, fought for their territories, mated, nested and prepared to bring forth the new cycle of life they had flown six or eight thousand miles to create. The male curlew fought insanely with every plover and sandpiper that crossed his territory boundary until the outer perimeters were flecked with the brown feathers of

trespassers that had retreated too slowly before the curlew's onslaughts. The mating hormones poured out by his glands could only dam up within him like an explosive charge.

Instinctively the curlew fought every other shorebird that ventured near, yet in his instinctive behavior pattern there was no enmity for the buntings, longspurs and ptarmigans that also occupied the tundra—birds not biologically related and not competitors for the same insect food he would need for his own nestlings when the female came. When a female willow ptarmigan built her nest and laid her

twelve buff eggs less than fifteen feet from the moss hummock where the curlew's nest would be, the curlew ignored
her and in a few days forgot she was there.

The nights grew darker and longer. The tiny, brilliant
flowers of the tundra dried into wisps of silk-plumed seed.
Close by, a pair of golden plover, their black bellies and
breasts glistening in the low rays of a morning sun, began
calling excitedly and flying in rapid circles. The curlew knew
their young had come, and like the young of all shorebirds,
already well developed at birth, they had left the nest and
were running about before the shells of the eggs that had
held them were dry. The Arctic summer was waning.

Several of the plovers' down-covered young scampered
into the curlew's territory and the mother followed them
with food. The curlew whistled a warning and flew toward
her. But the call of her young was stronger than the fear of
another much larger bird, and the plover stood her ground,
her wings spread protectively before the tiny, peeping balls
of yellow fluff which squirmed downwards into the mat of
reindeer moss. The curlew swerved upwards without striking her. And he didn't attack again. Instead he circled to a
rocky hummock a hundred feet away, alighted, watched the
plover feeding her young for a moment or two, and then
forgot her.

Within the curlew the annual rhythm of glandular activity had passed its peak and begun to ebb, and its product,
the belligerent drive of the mating time, was dying. A new
urge was replacing it. Where before, defense of the territory
was an overriding demand that took priority over even the
search for food, the curlew was now feeling the first stirrings

of a restless call to move. No female had come. The territory was losing its meaning.

Periodically the curlew flew back at the golden plover, but when the plover refused to fly the curlew would lose interest and forget her again. This went on for most of a day, the curlew suddenly remembering that there were intruders on his territory, then just as suddenly forgetting them. The next day other shorebirds moved in and out of the territory. Now the curlew ignored them. Once he flew far down river and was gone a couple of hours, the first time he had left the territory since arriving almost two months before.

Around him the young shorebirds of the year were maturing rapidly and their parents were abandoning them to fend for themselves. The disassociation between parents and young was abrupt and complete, the parents forming their own flocks, the young birds theirs.

It was late July. The tundra potholes and their muddy edges were teeming with the water insects and crustaceans on which the shorebirds fed. Food was at its peak of abundance and winter was still a couple of months away, but the Arctic had served its purpose and now the distant southland was calling the shorebirds flocks, many weeks before there was any real need for them to leave. The curlew who had fought savagely all summer to be alone, now felt a pressing desire for companionship.

There was no reasoning or intelligence involved. The curlew was merely responding in the ages-old pattern of his race to the changing cycle of physiological controls within him. As days shortened the decreasing sunlight reduced the activity of the bird's pituitary gland. The pituitary secretion was the trigger that kept the reproductive glands pouring sex hormones into the blood stream, and as the production of sex hormones decreased, the bird's aggressive mating urge disappeared and the migratory urge replaced it. It was entirely a physiological process. The curlew didn't know that winter was coming again to the Arctic and that insect eaters must starve if they remained. He knew only that once again an irresistible inner force was pressing him to move.

But somewhere in his tiny, rudimentary brain the simple beginnings of a reasoning process were starting. Why was he always alone? When the rabid fire of the mating time burned fiercely in every cell, where were the females of his species which the curlew's instinct promised springtime after springtime? And now with the time for the flocking come, why in the myriads of shorebirds and other curlews were there none of the smaller and lighter-brown curlews he could recognize as his own kind?

A few days later the lure of the territory disappeared entirely and the curlew rose high and flew southward for a couple of hours without alighting. He came down finally to feed on a small mudflat where a river emptied into a large lake. The tundra was now disgorging its summer population of shorebirds and flock after flock of southward moving sandpipers passed by. One flock of long-legged shorebirds, flying in a wavering V, swept low along the lakeshore. The curlew stopped his feeding and called excitedly, for the flight pattern and flock formation could only be curlew. The flock wheeled without breaking formation, moving with the precision and instantaneous timing of a single organism, as though one nerve centre controlled the movements of every bird. On stiffened, down-curved wings they glided in to the mudflat. The Eskimo curlew ran towards them, then stopped abruptly after a few strides and nonchalantly resumed his feeding. They were Hudsonian curlews with the shorter bills and buffy underparts which marked them as birds of this nesting.

The curlew didn't know that this other species, almost identical outwardly, was a slower flying bird unsuited as a

migration companion. He didn't know that young shore-birds of the year develop their full wing strength late and are left behind by the adults to follow by instinct the perilous 8,000-mile southward route they have never seen before. His instinctive behavior code, planted deep in his brain by the genes of countless generations, told him only what to do, without telling him why. His behavior was controlled not by mental decisions but by instinctive responses to the stimuli around him. He desired the association of a flock, but the Hudsonians had failed to release the flocking response in his inner brain and now he ignored them in his feeding. When they flew again a short time later, the Eskimo curlew hardly noted their departure. In a land pulsing with the wingbeats of migrating shorebirds, the curlew was alone again.

By afternoon the mudflat was dotted with the darting forms of shorebirds that had stopped to feed. Most of them kept together in flocks of their own species. At dusk the flocks ceased feeding and took off, one by one, until only the curlew remained, the birds of each flock whistling sibilantly to each other to retain formation in the falling darkness. They circled high until a half mile or so above the tundra, then leveled off and headed southward. It was usual for the shorebirds to migrate principally at night, for their digestion and energy consumption were rapid and the daylight was required for feeding. The high level of energy which migration demanded could be maintained only by timing the flights so that they ended with the dawn when feeding could be at once resumed.

Far above him, the curlew could hear the faint, lisping notes of the Arctic migrants pouring south to a warmer land. Needles of ice began forming at the shallow edges of the mudflat puddles. The bird's instinct rebelled at the idea of flying alone, yet when he called shrilly into the cold night there was no answer, and the time had come when he had to move.

He turned into the breeze, held his wings extended outward and adjusted the angle—leading edge up and trailing edge down—until he could feel the lifting pressure of the wind beneath them. Of all the shorebirds' wings, the Eskimo curlew's—long, narrow and gracefully pointed— were best adapted for easy, high-speed flight. Even standing motionless with wings extended in the faint, night breeze, the bird was weightless and almost airborne. He pushed off gently with his legs, took a few rapid wing-beats with the flight feathers twisted so that they bit solidly into the air, and rose effortlessly. He climbed sharply for more than a minute until the tundra almost vanished in the grey dark below, then he leveled off and picked up speed with a slower, easier wing-beat. The air rushed past him, pressing his body feathers tightly against the skin. The migration had begun. Even the curlew's simple brain sensed vaguely that the un-marked flyway ahead reaching down the length of two con-tinents was a long, grim gantlet of storm, foe and death.

Yet even now, before the austere flatlands of the Arctic had totally disappeared in the horizon mists behind him, the curlew was feeling the first faint stirrings of another year's mating call which would drive him back to await the female when springtime greened the Arctic lichens again.

...Being the hitherto unpublished notes of
Lucien Mc Shan Turner on the birds of Ungava...
I saw no Esquimaux curlew until the morning of
the 4th of September, 1884, as we were passing
out from the mouth of the Koksoak River. Here
an immense flock of several hundred individuals
were making their way to the south...

CHAPTER THREE

The curlew's wings beat with a strong, rapid, unchanging rhythm hour after hour. The strokes were deep, smooth and effortless, the wings sweeping low beneath his belly at every down-stroke and lifting high over the back with each return. Each stroke was an intricate series of gracefully co-ordinated actions merged with split-second precision into a single, smooth movement, for the curlew's wing was a wing and propeller combined. Each portion of the wing had a different flight role to play.

   The sturdy inner half next to the body deflected the air

stream as a kite or aircraft's wing does, so that pressure developed against the under surface and suction above— the "lift" that produces flight. It accomplished this by its aerodynamic shape alone. The flapping of the wings provided forward drive but had nothing to do with keeping the bird airborne.

The outer half of the curlew's wing, composed largely of the stiff, overlapping flight feathers, was the propeller that drove the bird forward, producing the air flow which gave lift to the inner wing. With every stroke, each individual feather in the outer half had to be twisted through a complex series of positions. With the down-stroke, the flight feathers twisted, front edges down and rear edges up, so that each feather was an individual propeller blade pushing air to the rear and driving the bird ahead. For the up-stroke, the angle of the feathers had to be reversed so that the push of the feathers against the air still produced a forward drive. The lift force of the inner wing was so powerful and constant that there was no loss of altitude on the up-stroke.

Each delicate adjustment of feathers was a reflex too rapid to be consciously controlled, for the curlew completed three or four wingbeats a second to give him a flight speed of fifty miles an hour.

Occasionally one of the curlew's wings would bite into the harder, spiraling air of a vortex left by the wingtips of a migrating shorebird ahead of him, for even the passage of another bird left a trail in the air that the curlew's delicately sensitized wings could detect. Usually this alteration in the air pattern was the curlew's first warning that he was overtaking a flock of birds ahead. When he found one of these vortexes, the curlew took advantage of it and followed it in with one wing riding the updraft edge of the horizontal column of spiraling air. In this way he found a degree of lift ready made for him and his own wings could work a little easier.

But no other shorebird except the golden plover flew as fast as the curlew did, and each time he slowly overtook the bird producing the vortex ahead. First he would hear the faint twitter of a flock's flight notes, the vortex would grow stronger, then the birds would appear as blurred figures against the grey sky in front. The curlew would fly with them for a time, but his greater speed would gradually drive him ahead. Then once more he would be flying alone.

This happened several times during the night, for the air layers close to the cooling tundra were turbulent and most of the shorebirds were flying at the same level just above the turbulence. Toward morning the curlew encountered another vortex trail and adjusted his wingbeat to the change in lift. He followed it for a long time and the vortex remained firm but grew no stronger. This time the curlew wasn't overtaking the flock ahead. Ducks and geese were not yet migrating, only two birds could be flying out of the Arctic now at a speed that the Eskimo curlew wouldn't rapidly overhaul. They had to be either golden plover or his own species, Eskimo curlew.

The curlew's tireless wings beat faster and the airflow pressed hard against his streamlined body. The wingtip vortex eddying back from the unseen flyers ahead strengthened, and it was a firmer, rougher vortex than any the curlew had encountered earlier in the night. It grew stronger almost imperceptibly, and the curlew's eagerness grew with it. A tenuous hope, part instinctive reaction and part a shadowy form of reasoning, formed nebulously in the curlew's brain. Was this the end of his lifelong quest for companions of his own kind? The curlew's wingbeat speeded until the powerful sinews of his breast muscles, gram for gram among the strongest of animal tissue on earth, pained with the strain.

The other birds were very close before their figures emerged, faintly at first and then more sharply, out of the darkness ahead. For a minute or more the curlew could detect only the vague, wavering lines of the flock's formation, then slowly the dark lines separated into individual birds. Only the fast, strong flyers like geese, curlew and golden plover flew in single-column, diagonally trailing lines or V's that permitted each bird to benefit from a wingtip vortex of the bird ahead yet escape the air turbulence directly behind it. And the curlew knew that the geese flocks were not yet migrating south. A restive excitement seized him and the curlew pushed on harder.

The gap closed rapidly and the birds ahead assumed sharper form. They were small, much smaller than the curlew, yet now there was not the instinctive rejection that had caused him to ignore the Hudsonian curlews and other shorebird flocks. The urge to join a flock was still as pressing as before. The curlew called out softly. Golden plovers answered.

It was a large group of forty or fifty, and the curlew moved in to a rearguard spot at the trailing end of one of the arms of the flock. He slackened flight speed and announced his presence with a rapid, twittering series of notes. The plovers answered again, the whole flock chattering sharply in unison. The curlew's flocking urge was satisfied. There was a vague, remote feeling of loneliness deep within him still, but the curlew was no longer alone.

Of the thirty-odd shorebirds which fly south out of the Canadian Arctic every fall, only the golden plover is suited as a migration companion for the Eskimo curlew. Their flight speeds and food preferences are similar, but there is another more important reason. With their tireless endurance as flyers, the golden plover and Eskimo curlew spurn the easy land route down the continent that all other migrating birds follow. Instead they work eastward to the rocky coasts of Labrador, Newfoundland or Nova Scotia, then strike out straight south over the Atlantic for a gruelling, non-stop flight of 2,500 or more miles which doesn't bring them to land again until they reach the northern shores of South America 48 hours later. Often a big Hudsonian godwit or, occasionally, a shorebird of some other species will join a golden plover flock and follow the plovers down the Atlantic on this long oversea short-cut south. But only the Eskimo curlew and golden plover do it regularly every fall, for only they, of all the Arctic's strong-winged shorebirds and waterfowl, possess the speed and power of flight to breast or escape the mid-ocean storms often encountered. The route enables them to take advantage of the rich crowberry crop that purples the hillsides and plateaus of the Labrador Peninsula each fall, a luxuriant store of food missed by the hosts of mid-continental migrants. But in spring the plovers and

curlew must follow the usual migratory route up the western plains. For then the crowberries are dead and hard beneath snows of the Labrador winter which linger for weeks after the mid-continent's Arctic is greening with spring.

Toward dawn the grey monotony of tundra, dimly visible far below, began to be pierced by slender, twisting fingers of black. The birds had covered four hundred miles since nightfall and were approaching the tree line where tundra gave way to the matted sub-Arctic forests of spruce. The black fingers reaching into the tundra were forested river valleys where stunted spruce thickets found shelter in the hollows against winter blizzards and precariously survived. With the first yellow-grey flush of dawn the flock dropped to a lakeshore mudflat, rested briefly, then as daylight came they began busily feeding.

The curlew with his stilt-like legs and long, downcurved bill stood out strikingly among the smaller, dark-plumaged, short-billed plovers. But the two birds, competitors and enemies on the nesting grounds, had migrated in company for countless generations and they mingled now as one species. Other shorebirds—yellowlegs, knots and the little semipalmated and least sandpipers—scurried close in their feeding, then withdrew. The curlew studied them closely, for somewhere in this vast Arctic tundra were birds he would recognize as his own kindred.

They fed all day with only occasional breaks for resting. With the darkness they flew again. The flock clung together loosely as they climbed for height, then as they leveled off the birds formed smoothly into a straggling V formation which permitted the inner wing of each bird to gain support from the whirling air produced by the outer wing of the bird ahead. The curlew took the lead position at the point of the V and the plovers fell in behind with a grace and ease as though the manoeuvre had been long practiced. No conscious selection of flock leader had taken place. The bird at the point position had to work harder to create lift and forward speed out of the unbroken air barrier ahead of it, and the curlew was the strongest flyer, so the remainder of the flock formed automatically behind in a movement as involuntary and spontaneous as each bird's breathing.

Soon after starting, the black fingers below merged into a solid mat. They were over spruce forest now and the tundra was behind. Other shorebirds were flying straight south toward the western plains, but the curlew led his flock southeastward, veering toward the matted crowberry vines of Labrador. Occasionally the curlew dropped back to an easier flight spot in the body of the flock, but each time after a brief rest he moved forward to the lead again.

PROCEEDINGS
of the
ACADEMY OF NATURAL SCIENCES
of Philadelphia
1861

August 13th. Dr. Leidy in the chair. Nine members present. The following papers were presented for publication: "On Three New Forms of Rattlesnakes," by Robert Kennicott. "Notes on the Ornithology of Labrador," by Elliott Coues . . .

The Esquimaux curlew arrived on the Labrador coast from its more northern breeding grounds in immense numbers, flying very swiftly in flocks of great extend, sometimes many thousands . . . the pertinacity with which they cling to certain feeding grounds, even when much molested, I saw strikingly illustrated on one occasion. The tide was rising and about to flood a muddy flat of perhaps an acre in extent, where their favorite snails were in great quantities. Although six or eight gunners were stationed on the spot, and kept up a continual round of firing upon the poor birds, they continued to fly distractedly about over our heads, notwithstanding the numbers that every moment fell. They seemed in terror lest they should lose their accustomed fare of snails that day . . .

By order of the library and publishing committee, the following proceedings of the Boston Society of Natural History for 1906-7 are published . . .

Paper no. 7—Birds of Labrador. By Charles W. Townsend, M.D., and Glover M. Allen . . . Numenius borealis (Forster), Eskimo curlew. Formerly an abundant but now a very rare autumn transient visitor in Labrador.

When August comes if on the Coast you be,
Thousands of fine Curlews, you'll daily see.

Packard writes of the curlew as follows: "On the 10th of August, 1860, the curlews appeared in great numbers. We saw one flock which may have been a mile long and nearly as broad; there must have been in that flock four or five thousand. The sum total of their notes sounded at times like the wind whistling through the ropes of a thousand-ton vessel . . ."

But we met with none during our visit to the Labrador coast in the summer of 1906. We talked with many residents and they all agreed that the curlew though formerly very abundant, suddenly fell off in numbers, so that now only two or three or none at all might be seen in a season. Capt. Parsons of the mailboat Virginia Lake said that they were very abundant up to thirty years ago. He often shot a hundred before breakfast, often killing twenty at a single discharge. Fishermen killed them by the thousands . . . they kept loaded guns at their fish stages and shot into the flying masses, often bringing down twenty or twenty-five at a discharge.

To sum up the evidence, we can state that the natives of Labrador persistently harassed the Eskimo curlew but did not realize that there was any diminution in their numbers until about 1888 to 1890. After 1892, but a small remnant of this formerly abundant bird has visited Labrador's shores . . . it is apparent that they are now a vanishing race—on the way to extinction.

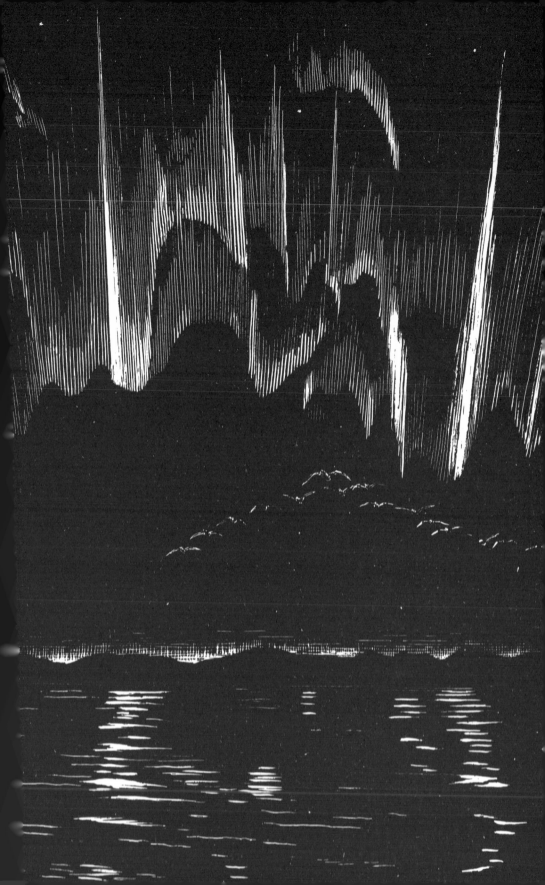

CHAPTER FOUR

Nights of endless flying and days of feeding at the edges of stagnant muskeg ponds followed monotonously. The green flashes of the Arctic sky's aurora borealis grew fainter behind them and they reached each dawn with hardening breast muscles that felt no fatigue. On the James Bay salt marshes food was abundant and they lingered for many days, gorging on the minute water and mud life until the southland call pressed them on again. The curlew led them straight eastward now over the ancient eroded mountains of Quebec

toward the gnarled gneiss seacliffs of Labrador's Gulf of St. Lawrence.

On the second morning the dawn came in foggy and cold. There was a sharp salty tang in the heavy air that struck their nostrils and the curlew led the flock on without stopping as the dawn brightened imperceptibly into a grey, sunless day. The air warmed and the fog banks thinned and here and there brown-green patches of the bare, craggy coastal plateau began appearing between the dispersing windrows of mist below them. Then the salt tang sharpened and the fog grew thick again and the curlew knew they were nearing the seacoast. There was nothing ahead, above or below but the pressing whiteness of fog, but the curlew held course unerringly. Suddenly, towards mid-morning, the enveloping whiteness was pierced by the rumble of surf and screeching of gulls. The curlew banked sharply and dropped in a steep dive, zigzagging erratically to control the speed of descent. The plovers broke their flock formation and followed the curlew down. They leveled off a feet above water, oriented themselves with the direction of wave movement and followed the wave crests in until the cliffs broke out of the fog in a giant rock wall that towered above them. The curlew had been flying blind for several hours, but he had overshot the coast by less than a mile.

They climbed again, skimmed across the cliff top and landed. Creeping, heath-like vines of the crowberry lay everywhere and in patches the fleshy, purple berries were so thick they hid the foliage. The birds commenced feeding immediately. The wind off the sea was cold and laden with fine rain. After an hour they stopped feeding and bunched together, each bird standing with its head into the gale so that the wind carried the rain back along its overlapping feathers and off its tail.

For two weeks now there would be nothing to do but gorge and fatten for the long, non-stop flight down the Atlantic to South America. It was mid-August and the Labrador summer was already almost gone. The nights were frosty; the days were days of interminable fog. They ate crowberries until their legs and bills and plumage and excrement were stained purple with the juice. On the odd day when the fog lifted under a warming sun they flew to the beaches at low tide periods to gorge on snails and shrimps.

Every day they encountered at least one other flock of golden plovers and the curlew would stop its feeding to scan the passing flocks for another curlew like himself. There were no other curlew, no other shorebirds of any species except the plovers. But other birds were numerous. Gulls, screeching raucously into the fog, were everywhere. Long black and white lines of eider ducks were passing endlessly offshore. The stubby-winged and clumsy-flying auks and murres were still gabbling and fighting on the cliff ledges where they had raised their summer broods.

Relatively inactive now, the curlew and plovers fattened quickly. Their breasts were soft and round again with the fat layers that covered the rigid muscles beneath. August had almost ended when the old restlessness seized them again. On days when the weather cleared and the wind was right thousands of other plovers climbed high and left the coastline on a course straight south across the Gulf of St. Lawrence toward the vast Atlantic beyond. But the curlew

waited, held by a tenuous bond that his meagre brain felt but couldn't quite identify. Vaguely he sensed that when the Eskimo curlews of the tundra came, they would have to come this way.

The restless urge to push on grew stronger and the curlew was torn between the two torturing desires—to wait and to move on. He found partial release from his rest-lessness by leading the flock on long flights up and down the coastline. Then the plovers began breaking away, joining in twos and threes with other southward flying plover flocks. The flock had dwindled to half is original size when September came and the nights grew suddenly colder. Now the fog banks which rolled in off the sea occasionally carried big,

wet flakes of snow. The last plover flocks had gone. The curlew's flock was alone with the gulls and eiders.

Frost had hardened the crowberries and with their succulent juices gone the feeding had become sparser. The fat that the birds had stored up as body fuel for their ocean flight was beginning to be re-absorbed before the flight had even begun.

Finally the curlew could restrain his migratory urge no longer. On a cold dusk after a blustery day during which the temperature had barely risen above the freezing point the curlew took wing and climbed into the murky sky. The cloud ceiling was low and the flock leveled off quickly and turned seawards into a strong head wind. At this altitude it was a full gale that cut their flight speed in half. Gusts periodically broke up the flock formation. Several weaker plov-

ers dropped behind. The curlew knew before the jagged
Labrador coastline was lost to sight behind that they couldn't
go on. He turned back and in a few minutes the flock alighted
again on a hillside lee where the gale whined distantly
overhead.

Having once started and failed, the curlew and plovers
were eager now to begin the long flight. But there were no
more false starts. The curlew waited restlessly for suitable
weather, but the season was now late and suitable days were
few. The fog dispersed but the south gale blew without
break for three days and three nights while the birds fed
intermittently on the drying crowberries and beach snails.
On the fourth day the gale swung around the compass and
continued, lighter now but colder, out of the north. This, a
tail wind, was as unfavorable as the head wind had been,
for it made balance in flight difficult and interfered with the
delicate reflex control of the broad outer wing feathers. The
north wind continued another three days, gradually weak-
ening, until dusk of the third day when it shifted westerly
and dropped to a faint breeze. This, a light cross wind, was
what the curlew awaited. Night came cold and clear.

The take-off, the climb for height, the automatic V-ing
with the curlew at the point were accomplished with the
same casual unthinking precision as on numerous dusks
before. The curlew and many of the plovers had made the
ocean flight in previous autumns and they had a shadowy,
remote memory of it. Most of them sensed obscurely that
when dawn came there would be only the vacant sea below
their wings, that they would fly on and on and another night
and another dawn would come and the same vacant sea

would still be there. And they knew that the sea was an alien and hostile element, for they were strictly creatures of the land and of the air. During periods of unusually smooth water they might alight briefly on the ocean's surface to snatch a few moments of rest, but they were clumsy swimmers at best, their feathers lacked oil and water-logged quickly, and rarely did the sea provide the calm conditions that would permit even a momentary landing. Usually the long flight, once begun, had to be completed non-stop without food for their stomachs or respite for their wings.

Behind them now the Arctic's aurora borealis was flashing vividly above the Labrador skyline, but when they came to earth again, with flight feathers frayed and their breast muscles numbed by fatigue, it would be in a dank jungle river-bottom of the Guianas or Venezuela. Yet there was no fear or hesitation now with the take-off, no recognition of the drama of the moment. There was only a vague relief to be off. For it was a blessing of their rudimentary brains that they couldn't see themselves in the stark perspective of reality—minute specks of earthbound flesh challenging an eternity of sea and sky.

For the increase and diffusion of knowledge among men. Smithsonian Institution, Washington. Annual Report of the Board of Regents for the year ending June 30, 1915. . . .

In Newfoundland and on the Magdalen Islands in the Gulf of St. Lawrence, for many years after the middle of the nineteenth century, the Eskimo curlews arrived in August and September in millions that darkened the sky. . . . In a day's shooting by 25 or 30 men as many as 2,000 curlews would be killed for the Hudson Bay Co.'s store at Cartwright, Labrador.

Fishermen made a practice of salting down these birds in barrels. At night when the birds were roosting in large masses on the high beach a man armed with a lantern to dazzle and confuse the birds could approach them in the darkness and kill them in enormous numbers by striking them down with a stick. . . .

CHAPTER FIVE

The curlew held to a course that was almost due south. When the tumbling Labrador hills dropped from sight behind, the last orienting landmark was lost, but the curlew led the flock unerringly on. Somewhere in the cosmic interplay of forces generated by the earth's rotation and magnetic field was a guide to direction to which hidden facets of his brain were delicately tuned. He held direction effortlessly, without conscious effort. An unthinking instinct, millenniums old, was performing subconsciously a feat beyond the ken of the highest consciousnesses in the animal world.

The night was but yet half spent when white surf outlined the craggy coastline of Nova Scotia's Cape Breton half a mile below. On some other years the curlew had stopped here, but the season was late and there was no thought of stopping now. It had taken five hours to cross the Gulf of St. Lawrence and the flock pushed now without pause across the tip of Cape Breton to the 2,500-mile misty maw of the Atlantic beyond.

The curlew dropped back for rest to an easier flight spot in the body of the flock and stayed there an hour while one of the plovers led. Then a cold front of air, moving eastward off the Canadian mainland, enveloped them in an area of turbulent air currents and the curlew moved forward to the lead again. The warm lower layers of air were being lifted by the heavier cold air pushing beneath. In the colder temperature of higher altitudes, the warm air's moisture began condensing, first into misty rain then, as its temperature dropped, it became snow.

Erratic air currents buffeted the flock and the formation broke up. The snow, light and sparse at first, became thicker. The flakes grew into large, loose, damp clusters that caked into the birds' wing feathers and made flight difficult. The curlew, reacting instinctively, led the flock upward in a steep spiraling climb. The air turbulence decreased as they climbed, but the snow clouds grew denser. The quieter air permitted them to line up in formation again, but they had to form ranks more by the feel of the wingtip air whorls than by sight, for now the snow was so thick that frequently even the bird next ahead was hidden. They stopped climbing and leveled off again.

There was no way of detecting how fast the cold front was moving eastward, but the curlew knew—partly from half-remembered experiences of previous migrations, but mostly by an instinctive intuition—that their 50-mile-an-hour flight speed would take them back through the front and keep them ahead of it, because the storm's front would be moving at a speed slower than theirs. But they would have to turn and fly with the storm, and that was eastward toward mid-Atlantic.

The curlew veered eastward and the double rank of plovers behind followed his deflecting air trail, though only the front few birds had been able to see the curlew turn. The snow clung to their wings, packed into the air slots between the flight feathers. Wings that a few minutes before had responded deftly to the gentle, rhythmic flexing of the breast muscles were now heavy and stiff, and they beat the air futilely like lifeless paddles, driving air downward in a waste of energy instead of deflecting it rearward for the horizontal airflow essential to flight. Their flight speed dropped until they were hovering almost motionless in a disorganized, bewildered cluster, now almost a mile above the sea. Then the curlew led them eastward again by angling slowly downward and drawing from gravitational pull the flight speed that their soggy wing feathers could no longer produce unaided. Now their flight speed was normal once more, but they were sacrificing altitude rapidly to maintain it. Up from the grey void below, the sea was rising steadily toward them.

The curlew led them on a long gradual, seaward incline, adjusting the downward flight angle to the pressure of the airflow on its sensitized wings so that normal speed was maintained with the minimum of altitude loss that would accomplish it. Occasionally the snow thinned and for brief intervals almost level flight was possible. Then it thickened again and their wings grew heavy and the curlew would have to angle sharply downward.

Behind them, but cut off probably by several flighthours of impenetrable snow, were the coastlines of Nova Scotia and New England. Ahead, perhaps only minutes, was the storm front with warmer undisturbed air before it. But even if the storm front were overtaken and passed there was only a limitless Atlantic beyond into which they would have to keep flying to stay ahead of the snow clouds now pressing them implacably towards the wavecrests below. All this the curlew knew, not from any process of reasoning but via the same nebulous channels of instinct which told him too that somewhere a mate of his own species was waiting for another breeding time to green the tundra lichens again.

Even the curlew's thick breast muscles and wing tendons, stronger by far than those of the smaller plovers he led, were aching and burning now from the abnormal energy output demanded to overcome the effect of the crusting snow on their wings. Their downward flight course took them into the lower layers of turbulent, bumpy air once more. The flock was thrown out of formation again. They clung together by calling sharply and constantly to each other. Each bird was alone in a gusty white world of its own, unseen and unseeing, but the quavering chatter of flight notes was a nexus that held them together.

For a long time the blind, numbing flight continued and the curlew fought to maintain height until not only his breast muscles but every fibre of his body throbbed with agonizing fatigue. To the lisping murmur of flight notes from the plovers behind there was soon added a sibilant hissing that came from below. The hissing grew stronger. It was the sound of snow striking water.

Then through the white curtain the curlew could see it. Waves with silvery caps curling upward appeared first ahead of the flock, paused momentarily below as they were overtaken, then disappeared behind. The snow had cleared slightly and now the plovers became visible again strung out haphazardly to the curlew's rear. The hindmost, weaker birds were lower, closer to the sea. They had had to sacrifice altitude faster to keep up with the stronger flyers ahead. Glutinous snow clung to their wingtips, the melting rate from body heat barely equalling the rate at which new snow accumulated.

The curlew would hold a level plane of flight for several seconds, then as forward speed decreased he would have to dip downward, gain new speed and level off again. The sea was clearly visible now, the white wave crests etched sharply against the black water. At times a higher crest leaped upward to within a few feet of the struggling birds.

A great wave appeared ahead. The curlew fought the lethargy in his wings and lifted over it painfully to drop into the trough beyond. He struggled on. The next crest was lower and the curlew mounted it with several feet to spare. Behind him, the great wave lunged into the plover flock. Three of the lower birds fought for height but could do no

more than hover helplessly. There was no cry. The wave
arched upward momentarily and the birds disappeared from
sight. The wave passed and the three plovers didn't re-
appear.

Nature, highly selective in all things, is most selective
with death. The weak neither ask nor obtain mercy.

The flock slogged on, a few feet above the sea, struggling
laboriously over each crest and snatching a few niggardly
seconds of partial rest in the quieter, protected air of each
trough. Once a long trough lifted into a seething comber
many feet higher than those preceding and the spray of its
crest lashed the curlew's wings. The curlew had to battle a
maelstrom of air currents for several seconds to keep airborne. When the wave passed two more of the plovers failed
to re-appear. But the spray melted much of the snow clinging to the curlew's wingtip feathers. For a minute his un-

burdened wings could bite into the air with all their old
power. Then the snow clogged them again. Only the knowledge that somewhere close ahead the cold front terminated
kept the curlew plunging on.

The air grew warmer very gradually, so slowly it was
difficult to detect the change. But the snow altered to rain
abruptly. At one wave crest there was only the swirling white
wall of snow ahead, by the next crest the snow was behind
and sheets of rain pelted them. The snow melted from their
feathers in a few seconds and the curlew led the remnant
of his flock upward in a sharp climb. The pain and fatigue
drained quickly from their wings and breasts with the re-
sumption of normal flight. The sea disappeared again in the
darkness beneath them. After several minutes they broke
through the rain front into a quiet mist-roofed world beyond.

... And sometimes, during northeast storms, tremendous numbers of the curlews would be carried in from the Atlantic Ocean to the beaches of New England, where at times they would land in a state of great exhaustion, and they could be chased and easily knocked down with clubs when they attempted to fly. Often they alighted on Nantucket in such numbers that the shot supply of the island would become exhausted and the slaughter would have to stop until more shot could be secured from the mainland.

The gunner's name for them was "dough-bird," for it was so fat when it reached us in the fall that its breast would often burst open when it fell to the ground, and the thick layer of fat was so soft that it felt like a ball of dough. It is no wonder that it was so popular as a game bird, for it must have made a delicious morsel for the table. It was so tame and unsuspicious and it flew in such dense flocks that it was easily killed in large numbers... two Massachusetts market gunners sold $300 worth from one flight... boys offered the birds for sale at 6 cents apiece... in 1882 two hunters on Nanutcket shot 87 Eskimo curlew in one morning... by 1894 there was only one dough-bird offered for sale on the Boston market.

CHAPTER SIX

The curlew knew that they had to continue flying eastward to keep the storm from overtaking them again, but it was a simple, uncolored, matter-of-fact knowledge. There was no lingering emotional reaction, no fear. The terrors of the snow-filled sky, the plovers forced into the sea, were forgotten almost immediately. Only the fact of the storm itself was remembered, and it was remembered not in panic or fright, but merely as a natural foe that was there and had to be avoided.

But their course eventually had to be southward, not

eastward. To the east for four thousand miles there was only empty sea. After half an hour the curlew turned the flock southward, and they flew south unhindered for almost another half hour before the eastward-moving storm front enveloped them again. At the first big drops of rain, the curlew veered sharply to the east once more and in a few minutes the flock re-entered clear air.

In the three hours that remained before dawn, they repeated this many times, flying south until the rain overtook them, then veering eastward to get ahead of it again. They were on a southerly course when the yellowing dawn pierced a murky eastern sky. Daylight came swiftly, changing the black of the sea to a cold green, but there was no sun. They flew southward for an hour, then two hours, and the cloud cover grew thinner and the day brightened and this time the storm didn't re-appear. Even the grey, bumpy clouds of the western sky vanished and in the east the sun cut like a torch through the dissolving mists. The air remained cold, but in a short time the sun stood alone in a blue and otherwise empty sky.

The birds had worked southward around the storm. The snow clouds of the night, what would be left of them, would be breaking up now far to the north over the codfish shoals of Newfoundland's Grand Banks.

In mid-morning the air warmed and eddying wisps of fog began rising off the sea. The sky above remained blue and clear, but at times the sea below was completely hidden by layers of mist. They were approaching the spot where the icy Labrador current flowing southward out of the Arctic met the tepid northward-flowing tropic waters of the Gulf

Stream. Here the Gulf Stream is deflected eastward past New-foundland into mid-Atlantic. After an hour of intermittent fog the sea lay bare again. Then its pale green Arctic waters changed abruptly to a deep indigo blue with a line of de-marcation as sharp as a line between water and shore. They were over the Gulf Stream, a product of the tropics. The green of the Labrador current, last feature of the Arctic, faded behind them.

Their wings beat mechanically, without change of pace or fatigue. The air warmed constantly, for each hour put them fifty miles southward. The only change in the drowsy monotony of flight came when, at intervals, they let them-selves drop low to skim the wavetops for perhaps an hour before climbing again.

At low altitude the sea, like the Arctic tundra, revealed that its surface mask of lifeless barrenness was illusion. Life was there, abundantly, when the birds came low enough to see it. At times shimmering discs of jellyfish dotted the sea for miles; the sun glinted metallically off a thousand silver flanks as schools of small fish darted upward into the surface layers; and sometimes there were clouds of minute one-celled plankton creatures, each one a microscopic grain of orange pigment by itself, but in their billions they colored miles of sea a vivid red.

Down close to the water, there were other birds too, birds that spent most of their lives skimming the open vistas of sea, touching land only when the irresistible urge of the nesting time drove them ashore. Wilson's petrels fluttered moth-like and dodged erratically between wave crests, their white rumps flashing like tiny breakers as they fed incessantly on the sea's crustacea and plankton. Phalaropes which had nested on the Arctic tundra with their shorebird kin had returned now to the sea which would lure them until another nesting time came. Occasionally a bigger shear-water soared past on black, motionless wings that skilfully utilized the updrafts created atop each wavecrest by the upward deflection of surface wind. But these were true birds of the sea. The sea gave them food, and when their wings tired the sea also gave them rest, for they swam as skilfully as they flew.

The curlew and plovers could only keep flying, waiving food and rest until the landfall came.

By evening they had crossed the eastward-flowing arm of the Gulf Stream and were over the immense two-million-square-mile eddy of the mid-Atlantic where no currents came to stir the brackish water and where the rubbery fronds of sargassum weed collected in the great floating islands of the Sargasso, weirdest of all seas. They had flown almost twenty-four hours, yet there was no fatigue in the pulsing muscles of their breasts.

Vast meadows of brown floating algae passed beneath. At intervals when the birds came low, they would see flying fish with great wing-like pectoral fins extended, skimming over the soggy knots of seaweed. There were crabs, shrimps and sea snails clinging to the seaweed stems. In other years this first dusk had put the curlew within sight of Bermuda's flat-topped Sear's Hill, but the night's storm had driven them far to the eastward, and now the sun set in an empty sea. When darkness came, the sea flamed with the cold white light of millions of phosphorescent creatures.

The curlew led the flock upward and throughout the night they flew steadily at a height of a half mile or so, the birds calling intermittently to each other. When the curlew was leading the flock his senses had to be kept sharply tuned to the vagaries of wind and the cosmic impulses which his brain interpreted into a sense of direction. When he dropped back for rest, he could fly in a half-sleep, his wings beating automatically, his eyes half shut, following subconsciously the trailing air vortex of the bird ahead of him.

That night the North Star and the familiar constellations of the Arctic sky dropped almost to the northern horizon. New star groups rose to the south. And shortly before dawn the wind freshened, a warm, firm wind that blew with monotonous constancy out of the northeast. They had entered the region of the trade winds. It was a quartering tail wind that gave them almost another ten miles an hour of speed.

Day, when it came, was hot despite the wind. Occasionally the grey-blue form of a shark glided close to the sea's surface. This was the rim of the tropics, and the sea turned bluer, and condensation of the hot rising air gave the sky a lumpy patchwork of white cumulus clouds. The cloud shadows dappled the blue water with constantly changing patterns of grey. Occasionally there were thicker knobs of cloud that hung motionless on the western horizon, the island signposts of the sea, for every island had its cap of cloud that was visible far beyond the island's own horizons. These were the Lesser Antilles of the outer Caribbean. And far beyond the rim of the sea, ahead, another twelve hours of flying away, were the jungles and mountains of South America.

Now their breasts and wing tendons were tiring from the thirty-six hours of flying behind them. Flight was no longer the effortless subconscious reflex it had been. It had become a function that had to be willed, only conscious concentration on the task kept their flagging wings working. Two nights and a day without food had slowed their body processes. Now they had to pant rapidly in the hot tropic air, their bills slightly agape, to capture the oxygen supply their lungs demanded. Three of the plovers, one-year-olds making the long ocean flight for the first time, dropped slowly behind and the curlew at the point of the flock slowed to a flight speed that the weaker birds could maintain.

The curlew knew that where the thick clouds dotted the western horizon there were islands only an hour or

two's flight away. But to reach them would require a course that would put the wind directly on their tails, and a wind from straight behind could interfere with flight as seriously as a wind from dead ahead. So the curlew held to the original course. And he knew that long before the coast could be reached a third night would be upon them. Then the landfall would come in darkness and if the night were cloudy and black there could be no landing even then until the dawn light revealed the outlines of Venezuela's mangrove swamps and river sand-bars.

The day passed with interminable slowness, the sun sank finally into the Caribbean and the night dropped quickly without twilight. Then the overcast moved in to shut out

moon and stars, and rain began falling, for they were reaching the tropics at the height of the rain season. But it was a light, fine rain that cooled the air and made breathing easier. And it was a signal that the coast was approaching.

For another two hours they flew through rain. The curlew could see nothing, but he knew immediately when they left the sea and were flying over land. First the rumble of surf came up through the darkness, then the air became turbulent with the thermal updrafts lifting off the warmer land.

They could do nothing but fly on for hours longer. And now, with the knowledge that land lay below, the continuance of flight became the harshest ordeal of all. Every wingbeat was a torturing battle with lethargy and fatigue. And much of the energy used was now wasted, for their flight feathers were frayed and ragged, no longer capable of the sharp propelling bite of feather against air which had made flights so easy and effortless when they left Labrador.

The curlew knew that once they had crossed the coastal strip with its beaches and river estuaries, there was nothing beyond for a hundred and fifty miles but the dense tangle of mangrove swamp where a landing was as impossible as on the open sea. Now, even if the night cleared, they would have to push on regardless until the flat, grassy llanos of the Venezuelan interior spread out below them. Despite the growing heaviness of their wings, the curlew led them upward to clear the coastal mountains he knew were ahead. The climb was a torturing anguish. They leveled off, but it brought no respite to the burning pangs of fatigue which throbbed in every fibre of their small bodies.

The night remained black. At last the dawn came, not yellow or red, but in a sombre pall of greyness. The land below was a drowned and sodden land of mud, water and swollen rivers, like the springtime tundra of the Arctic. The broad treeless valley of the great Orinoco spread in every direction as far as the grey pall would let them see. The rain still fell.

They had flown without rest or food for almost sixty hours. From a land of snow and the northern lights, they had come non-stop to a land that was steaming with the rank growth of the tropics. Below them were hundreds of miles of mudflats and grassy prairie that teemed with the abundance of aquatic insect food that only the months of tropical rain could produce.

With the first misty light of the dawn, the curlew arched his stiffened wings and plunged downward in an almost vertical dive. He had spanned the length of a continent since his wings had last been still. The plovers followed. The flock touched down.

But not a bird rested, for feeding had to come first. Their stomachs had been empty fifty-five hours and they had flown close to three thousand miles on the fuel stored in Labrador as body fat. Now the fat was gone and in less than three days each bird had lost ten to fifteen per cent of its weight. Only the fact that they were the most economical fuel users in the animal world had made the flight possible. Each bird had burned about two ounces of fat over the ocean—at the same rate of fuel consumption, a half ton plane would fly one hundred and sixty miles on a gallon of fuel instead of the usual twenty miles.

They fed rapidly until mid-morning, and only then did they rest. On the broad savannahs abutting the Orinoco, food was abundant. They fed again for several hours before the first tropic night brought darkness.

This is the eighth in a series of bulletins of the United States National Museum on the Life Histories of North American Birds by Arthur Cleveland Bent. Order Limicolae. Family Scopopacidae ... Numenius borealis, Eskimo curlew ... excessive shooting on its migrations and in its winter home in South America was doubtless one of the chief causes of its destruction ... I cannot believe that it was overtaken by any great catastrophe at sea which could annihilate it; it was strong of wing and could escape from or avoid severe storms; and its migration period was so extended that no one storm could wipe it out. There is no evidence of disease or failure of food supply. No, there was only one cause, slaughter by human beings, slaughter in Labrador and New England in summer and fall, slaughter in South America in winter and slaughter, worst of all, from Texas to Canada in the spring. They were so confiding, so full of sympathy for their fallen companions, that in closely packed ranks they fell, easy victims of the carnage. The gentle birds ran the gantlet all along the line and no one lifted a finger to protect them until it was too late . . .

CHAPTER SEVEN

The plovers and curlew lingered on the savannahs of the Orinoco for two weeks, rapidly growing fat again. There were thousands of other shorebirds flocking the great grasslands—golden plovers that had come down the long oceanic migration route as the curlew's flock had done, and a dozen other species that had followed the land route of the central plains and the Panama Isthmus to rendezvous here on the Venezuelan prairies. There were brilliant tropical birds too, now in the middle of their nesting time and busily feeding young. White egrets had covered acres of riverside swamp with their big nests, the nests often so numerous that they touched one another. Flocks of scarlet ibis, the gems of tropical bird life, followed the river banks in their food hunts, approaching first as silhouettes of colorless grey, then flaming into a vivid scarlet as they came nearer, and fading to grey again when they passed.

Food was limitless on the llanos, and many of the Arctic shorebirds would migrate no farther, but after two weeks of feeding had fattened them once more the curlew and plover felt the old restless torment calling them again to a more distant southland. The other plover flocks had already gone. As in Labrador, the curlew's flock was the last to depart.

They took off on a bright moonlit night early in October, followed a tributary valley of the Orinoco until it lost itself in the mountain range which separated the Orinoco and Amazon watersheds, then dropped into a deep valley of one of the Amazon's tributaries beyond. They followed the slender thread of water southward, and by dawn they had reached the broad Amazon itself. Here, south of the equator, the trade winds had switched from northeast to southeast, and, in order to fly with a beam wind, that next night they turned southwest instead of south. Another five hundred miles of flying that night put them, by dawn, within sight of the Peruvian Andes' snow-capped peaks. The wind here on the southern fringe of the trades was easterly, and for three nights following they flew southeast. On the fifth dawn, gaunt and wing-worn again, they dropped to the grassy flatlands of the Argentine pampas, twenty-five-hundred miles south of the Venezuelan llanos.

Spring was greening the pampas-grass and giant thistle. Grasshoppers were emerging. For days the birds did little but gorge on the insect life of the short grass plains, flying at intervals to the lower levels where the grass grew denser in brackish marshes and swarms of aquatic insects provided a change of diet. They were always moving, but never moving far. Their worn wing feathers were moulted one by one and replaced, giving them full flight power again. Here, they were eight thousand miles from the Arctic nesting grounds and of all the tundra shorebirds species only the yellowlegs, knot, buff-breasted sandpiper and one or two others had migrated so far, yet at times the restless migration urge still pressed the curlew and plovers southward. On clear nights when the prevailing westerlies swept strongly across the prairies, giving them a good beam wind, the flock would take off again. Hours later, another one or two hundred miles southward, the restlessness would be temporarily appeased and the curlew would lead them down to a moonlit knoll to await the dawn.

In this manner they straggled slowly southward. By the time the hot December sun had burned the giant thistles, and the pampas-grass was silver with its nodding panicles of flowers, they were deep down into the stony undulating plains of Patagonia, within a single night's flight of the Antarctic Sea. The herculean thrust of the migratory impulse had carried them from the very northernmost to the southernmost reaches of the mainland of the Americas. Yet even here there were still great flocks of shorebirds. The days were long and hot, the brief nights cool. Of all the world's living creatures, none but the similarly far-flying Arctic tern sees as much sunlight as the shorebirds which spend each year chasing, almost pole to pole, the lands of the midnight sun.

For almost five months the curlew and plovers had been goaded by an insatiable drive that had relaxed at times but never fully disappeared. Now the urge of the migration time was dead. A peculiar lethargy gripped the plovers and they were content to fly back and forth between two salt lagoons—feeding, dozing, flying listlessly, waiting like an actor who has forgotten his lines for the prompting of instinct to tell them what to do next.

But within the curlew, as fast as the pressure of the migratory urge relaxed a new tormenting pressure replaced it. It was the old vague hunger and loneliness. Suddenly the curlew remembered again that he lived alone in a world to which other members of his own species never came. A restlessness of a different sort beset him. He tried to lead the plovers farther afield but they would not follow. Finally the restlessness became irresistible. The curlew spiraled high, circled and re-circled the lagoon where the plovers were feeding. He called loudly and repeatedly, but the plovers gave no sign of hearing. Then the curlew turned eastward toward the coastal tide flats that he knew were there, many hours of flight away. He was flying alone again.

Patagonia had none of the deep rich soil of the pampas. Much of it was gravelly shingle, cut by sharp ridges of volcanic rock, and the vegetation was scanty. Even where the coarse grass and thistles grew, they were burned brown now by the fierce summer sun. Out of this arid land the shorebirds were drifting eastward toward the cool, food-rich mudflats of the seacoast.

Here one of the highest tides of the world leaves miles of beach exposed at every ebb, and the stranded flotsam of the sea replenished twice daily was a food supply that never waned. Vast flocks followed each low tide outward. Most of them were golden plover, but there were yellowlegs too, flashing their white rumps, while buff-breasts and sanderlings daintily dodged the breakers as though afraid to get their feet wet.

The curlew wandered from flock to flock, searching restlessly he was not sure what. His long, down-curved bill and wide spread of wing made him stand out prominently among the thousands of other smaller shorebirds.

It was January, and the tundra nine thousand miles to the north would remain for months yet a sleeping, lifeless land of blizzard and unending night, but the curlew began to feel the Arctic's first faint call. It was a feeble stirring deep within, a signal that dormant sex glands were awakening again to another year's breeding cycle. It was barely perceptible at first. It strengthened slowly. And it was a sensation vastly different from the autumn migratory urge. The call to migrate south had been a vague, restless yearning for movement in which the goal was only dimly defined, but in this new call the goal was everything and the migration itself would be incidental. The essence of what the curlew felt now was a nostalgic yearning for home. And the goal was explicit—not merely the Arctic, not the tundra, but that same tiny ridge of cobblestone by the S-twist of the river where the female would come and the nest would be.

The curlew started home. Drifting slowly from mudflat to mudflat, he didn't move far each day, but the aimlessness was gone. The movement was always northward.

The other shorebirds had felt it too. They were constantly moving and the bird population of the mudflats changed with every hour. In a week the curlew was two hundred miles northward.

The object of the general appendix to the annual report of The Smithsonian Institution is to furnish brief accounts of scientific discovery in particular directions; reports of investigations made by collaborators of the institution . . .

The Eskimo curlew and its disappearance (Reprinted in this annual report after revision by the author, Myron H. Swenk, from the proceedings of The Nebraska Ornithologists' Union, Feb. 27, 1915.)

It is now the consensus of opinion of all informed ornighologists that the Eskimo curlew (Numenius borealis) is at the verge of extinction, and by many the belief is entertained that the few scattered birds which may still exist will never enable the species to recoup its numbers, but that it is even now practically a bird of the past. And, judging from all analogous cases, it must be confessed that this hopeless belief would seem to be justified, and the history of the Eskimo curlew, like that of the passenger pigeon, may simply be another of those ornithological tragedies enacted during the last half of the nineteenth century, when because of a wholly unreasonable and uncontrolled slaughter of our North American bird life several species passed from an abundance manifested by flocks of enormous size to a state of practical or complete annihilation ...

The Committee on Bird Protection desires to present herewith to the fifty-fifth stated meeting of the American Ornithologists' Union the results of its inquiries during 1939 into the current causes of depletion or maintenance of our bird life ... but the most dangerously situated are unquestionably the California condor, Eskimo curlew and ivory-billed woodpecker. They have been reduced to the point where numbers may be so low that individuals remain separated thus interfering critically with reproduction ...

CHAPTER EIGHT

The arrival of the female was a strangely drab and undra-
matic climax to a lifetime of waiting. One second the curlew
was feeding busily at the edge of the breakers, surrounded
by dozens of plovers, yet alone; the next second the female
curlew was there, not three feet away, so close that when
she held her wings extended in the moment after landing
even the individual feathers were sharply distinguishable.
She had come in with a new flock of nine plovers. They had
dropped down silently, unnoticed except by the sentinel
plover that stood hawk watch while the others fed. She

lowered her wings slowly and deliberately, a movement much more graceful than the alighting pattern of the plovers. Her long, downward sweeping bill turned toward him.

The female bobbed up and down jerkily on her long greenish legs and a low, muffled *quirking* came deep from within her throat. The male bobbed and answered softly.

There was little mental reasoning involved in the process of recognition. It was instantaneous and intuitive. The male knew that he had been mistaken many times before. He knew that the puzzlingly similar Hudsonian curlews were far to the north, wintering on the shores of the Caribbean, and that only another Eskimo curlew could be this far south. He knew this new curlew was smaller and slightly browner, like himself, than the others had been. But these thoughts were fleeting, barely formed. It was a combination of voice, posture, the movements of the other bird, and not her appearance, which signaled instantly that the mate had come.

He had never seen a member of his own species before. Probably the female had not either. Both had searched two continents without consciously knowing what to look for. Yet when chance at last threw them together, the instinct of generations past when the Eskimo curlew was one of the Americas' most abundant birds made the recognition sure and immediate.

For a minute they stood almost motionless, eyeing each other, bobbing occasionally. The male seethed with the sudden release of a mating urge that had waxed and waned without fulfillment for a lifetime. A small sea snail crept through a shallow film of tidewater at his feet and the curlew snapped it up quickly, crushing the shell with his bill. But he didn't eat it himself. With his neck extended, throat feathers jutting out jaggedly and legs stiff, the male strutted in an awkward sideways movement to the female's side and handed her the snail with his bill. The female hunched forward, her wings partly extended and quivering vigorously. She took the snail, swallowing it quickly.

In this simple demonstration of courtship feeding, the

male had offered himself as a mate and been accepted. The love-making had begun. There had been no outward show of excitement, no glad display, simply a snail proffered and accepted, and the mating was sealed.

Now they resumed feeding individually, ignoring each other, but never straying far apart. And the cobble bar by the S-twist of the distant tundra river called the male as never before.

At dusk he took wing and circled over the female, whistling to her softly. She sprang into the air beside him and together they flew inland over the coastal hills. They landed on a grassy hillside when darkness fell and they slept close together, their necks almost touching. The male felt as if he had been reborn and was starting another life.

They returned to the beaches at dawn and began to move northward more rapidly, alternating flights of ten miles or so at a time with stops for feeding. The call of the tundra grew more powerful and each day they moved faster than the day before, flying more and eating less. By early February they were a thousand miles north of where they had started, still following the seacoast tideflats, and the springtime turgescence of the sex glands with their outpouring of hormones began filling them with a growing excitement. Now the male would frequently stop suddenly while feeding and strut like a game cock before the female with his throat puffed out and tail feathers expanded into a great fan over his back. The female would respond to the love-making by crouching, her wings aquiver, and beg for food like a young bird. Then the male would offer her a food tidbit and their bills would touch and the love display suddenly end.

One dusk when the westerly wind was strong off the coastal highlands, they flew inland as they had done every evening, but this time the male led her high above the browning pampas and darkness came and they continued flying. The short daytime flights were not carrying them northward fast enough to appease the growing migratory urge. They left the seacoast far behind and headed inland northwesterly toward the distant peaks of the Andes. Now the male felt a sudden release of the tension within him, for with the first night flight there was recognition that the migration had really begun.

They flew six hours and their wings were tired. It was still dark when they landed, to rest till the dawn. Now they moved little during the day, but at sunset the curlew led his mate high into the air and turned northwestward again. Each night their wings strengthened and in a week they were flying from dusk to dawn without alighting.

They flew close together, the male always leading, the female a foot or two behind and slightly aside riding the air vortex of one of his wingtips. They talked constantly in the darkness, soft lisping notes that rose faintly above the whistle of air past their wings, and the male began to forget that he had ever known the torture of being alone. They encountered numerous plovers but their own companionship was so complete and satisfying that they made no attempt to join and stay with a larger flock. Usually they flew alone.

The northward route through South America was different from the southward flight. When they left the belt of the prevailing westerlies and passed over the pampas into the forested region of northern Argentina, feeding places became more difficult to find. Five hundred miles to the west were the beaches of the Pacific but the towering cordillera of the Andes lay between. They were entering the region of the southeast trades and to keep the wind abeam they could fly northeastward into the endless equatorial jungles of Brazil where food and even landing places would be scarce for fifteen hundred miles, or they could swing westward to challenge the high, thin, stormy air of the Andes which had the coastal beaches of the Pacific just beyond. The curlew instinctively turned westward.

For a whole night they flew into foothills which sloped upward interminably, climbing steadily hour after hour until their wings throbbed with the fatigue. And at dawn, when they landed on a thickly grassed plateau, the rolling land ahead still sloped upward endlessly as far as sight could reach, to disappear eventually in a saw-toothed horizon where white clouds and snow peaks merged indistinguishably.

When the sun set, silhouetting the Andean peaks against a golden sky, the curlews flew again. Flight was slow and labored for the angle of climb grew constantly steeper. The air grew thin, providing less support for their wings and less oxygen for their rapidly working lungs. They were birds of the sea level regions and they didn't possess the huge lungs which made life possible here three miles above the sea for the shaggy-haired llamas and their Indian herders. The curlews tired quickly and hours before dawn they dropped exhausted to a steep rocky slope where a thin covering of moss and lichen clung precariously. For the

remainder of the night they stood close together resting, braced against the cold gusty winds.

Daylight illuminated a harsh barren world, a vertical landscape of grey rock across which wisps of foggy cloud scudded like white wings of the unending wind. And the top of this world was still far above them. The peaks that they yet had to cross were hidden in a dense ceiling of boiling cloud. Nowhere else in the world outside the Himalayas of India did mountain peaks rear upward so high.

Even here, though, there were insects and the curlews fed. It was slow and difficult feeding, not because food was scanty, but because every movement was a tiring effort, using up oxygen that the blood regained slowly and pain-fully. At dusk the air cooled suddenly and the fog scud changed to snow. They didn't fly. The turbulent air currents and the great barrier of rock and glacier ahead demanded daylight for the crossing.

There was no sleep, even little rest, that night. The wind screeched up the mountain face, driving hard particles of snow before it, until at times the birds could hardly stand against it. Then a heavy blast lifted them off their feet and catapulted them twisting and helpless into dark and eerie space. The male fought against it, regained flight control and landed again. But the female was gone.

He called frantically above the whine of the storm but his calls were flung back unanswered by the wind. When the wind eased, he rose into the air and flew in tight, low circles, searching and calling, in vain. The wind rose, became too strong for flight, and he clung to the moss of the steep rock face and waited breathlessly. When it died momentarily, he flew again, but his endurance waned quickly and he couldn't go on. He found a hollow where he could be sheltered from the storm and crouched in it, panting with open bill for the oxygen his body craved. When strength returned he flew out into the wild dark night another time, circling, call-ing, the agony of loneliness torturing him again.

In an hour he found her, crouched in the drifting snow beneath a shelf of shale, as breathless and distraught as he

was. They clung together neck to neck and the heat of their bodies melted a small oval in the hard granular snow.

The wind slackened at dawn and the male knew they had to fly, for there could be no lingering here. When the snow changed to fog again and the sun pierced it feebly in a faint yellow glow, they took off and spiraled upwards into the flat cloud layer that hid the peaks above. In a minute they were entombed in a ghostly world of white mist which pressed in damp and heavy upon them. They spiraled tightly, climbing straight upward into air so thin that their wings seemed to be beating in a vacuum and their lungs when filled still strained for breath.

In the cloud layer the air was turbulent. Occasionally there were pockets where the air was hard, and their wings bit into it firmly and they climbed rapidly, then the air would thin out again, and for several minutes they would barely hold their own. Once the light brightened and the curlew knew they were close to the clear air above, but before they could struggle free of the cloud a sudden downdraft caught them, they plunged downward uncontrollably and lost in a few seconds the altitude that had taken many minutes to gain.

They broke free of the swirling cloud mass finally and came out into a calm, clear sky. It was a weird, bizarre world of intense cold and dazzling light which seemed disconnected from all things of earth. The cloud layer just below them stretched from horizon to horizon in a great white rolling plain that looked firm enough to alight upon. The sun glared off it with the brilliance of a mirror. A mile away a mountain peak lifted its cap of perpetual snow through the cloud, its rock-ribbed summit not far above. In the distance were other peaks rising like rocky islands out of a white sea.

The curlews leveled off close to the cloud layer and flew toward the peak. Flight was painful and slow. They flew with bills open, gasping the thin air. Their bodies ached.

As they approached the mountain top, the wind freshened again. Stinging blasts of snow swirled off the peak into their path of flight. They struggled through and landed for rest on a turret of grey rock swept bare of snow by the

wind. Now a new torment racked their aching bodies, for the dry, rarified air had quickly exhausted body moisture, and their hot throats burned with thirst.

Fifty miles away there were orchids and cacti blooming vividly in the late South American summer, but here on the rooftop of the Americas four miles above the level of the sea was winter that never ended. Not far below their resting place was an eerie zone of billowing white in which it was difficult to distinguish where the snow of the mountainside ended and the clouds began. Yet even here where no living thing could long endure, life had left its mark, for the very rock of the mountain itself was composed largely of the fossilized skeletons of sea animals that had lived millions of years ago, in a lost aeon when continents were unborn and even mountain peaks were the ooze of the ocean floors.

The pain drained from their bodies and the curlews flew westward again past the wind-sculptured snow ridges and out into the strangely unattached and empty world of dazzling sunlight and cloud beyond. They flew a long time, afraid to drop down through the cloud again until there was some clue as to what lay below it, and far behind them the peak grew indistinct and fuzzy beneath its halo of mist and snow. The cloud layer over which they flew loosened, its smooth, firm top breaking up into a tumbling series of deep valleys and high white hills. The valleys deepened, then one of them dropped precipitously without a bottom so that it wasn't a valley but a hole that went completely through the cloud. Through the hole, the birds could see a sandy, desert-like plateau strewn with green cacti clumps and brown ridges of sandstone. It was two to three miles below them, for the Andes' western face drops steeply to the Pacific.

They had been silent all day, for the high altitude flight took all the energy their bodies could produce, but now

103

the male called excitedly as he led the female sharply down-ward between the walls of cloud. The narrow hole far below grew larger. The air whistled past them and they zigzagged erratically to check the speed of the descent. At first the air was too thin to give their wings much braking power and they plunged earthward with little control, then the air grew firmer, it pressed hard against their wing feathers and they dropped more slowly. Their ears pained with the change in pressure and when they came out below the cloud layer they leveled off again and headed toward the faint blue line of the Pacific visible at the horizon.

Their brief two or three minutes of descent had brought them with dramatic suddenness into a region greatly dif-ferent from the cold, brilliant void they had left. They were still so high that features below were indistinct, but they were nevertheless a definite part of the earth again. Now there was land and rock and vegetation below them, not an ethereal nothingness of cloud. Here the day was dull and sunless, not glaring with light, but the air was warm. And the air now had a substance that could be felt. It gave power and lift to their wings again and it filled their lungs without leaving an aching breathless torment when exhaled.

They flew swiftly now, for the land sloped steeply and their plane of flight followed the contour of the land down-ward. Late that afternoon they alighted on a narrow beach of the Pacific. They drank hurriedly of the salt water for a couple of minutes. Then they fed steadily until the dusk.

With twilight the sky cleared and the great volcanic cones of the Andes, now etched sharply against the greying east, assumed a frightening massiveness. Every year the male curlew's migratory instinct had led him across this towering barrier of limestone, storm and snow. And every year before the memory of it dimmed, the curlew looked back and even his slow-working brain could marvel at the endurance of his own wings.

The Committee on Bird Protection fears that the following species must be placed on the list of those whose survival is doubtful: the California condor (less than fifty birds surviving); ivory-billed woodpecker (less than thirty birds known); Eskimo curlew (population—if any—unknown)...

No additional information on the Eskimo curlew is available. It is of course quite possible that the bird is extinct, but the few reports of its existence during the past decade lead one to hope that it has been merely overlooked by observers. It would seem advisable, however, for the American Ornithologists' Union to attempt to establish relationships with organizations or persons in Argentina and perhaps other South American republics that might be in a position to make investigations. If curlews were found to be wintering in that country it is possible that through the Argentine National Park directors or other means, some steps might be taken to assure better protection . . .

CHAPTER NINE

For nine months of migration each year the curlews were the pawns on a great two-continent chessboard and the players that decided the moves were the cosmic forces of nature and geography—the winds, tides and weather. Winds determined the direction the birds would fly. Tides and rainfall, by controlling the availability of food, determined each flight's goal. Now another player, an ocean current, entered the game.

The Pacific's massive Humboldt current which sweeps northward from the Antarctic along South America's western coast carries icy water almost to the equator. The onshore breezes which each afternoon blow in to the Peruvian coast are dry winds for there is little evaporation of moisture from the cold Humboldt water. So the narrow coastal strip between the Andes and the sea is a parched region of sandy desert plateaus where rain rarely falls. Few rivers tumble down the Andes' western slopes into the Pacific to create the estuary mudflats on which the tides can scatter the food-stuffs of the sea for the shorebird flocks. So here the shor-ebirds eat sparsely. They are tired and thin after the high Andes crossing but the coastal deserts conceived in the Humboldt's Antarctic water drive them on without rest.

The curlews followed the narrow Peruvian beaches northward, flying hard each night until the dawn, using every hour of daylight in the wearying search for food. They were always tired and never fully fed. There was neither time nor energy now for the courtship displays, little time even for rest.

In less than a week they covered two thousand miles and reached the sandy flatlands of Punta Parinas near the equator, where the South American coast turns back north-eastward toward its juncture a thousand miles away with the Isthmus of Panama.

March was almost here. Far to the north, spring would be moving up the Mississippi Valley, greening the cotton-woods and prairie grasses. The curlews were still south of the equator, the tundra was still six thousand miles away. Now the Arctic beckoned with a fever and fierceness that their aching and wasted breast muscles couldn't still.

Here the coast swung in a great twenty-five-hundred-

mile crescent east, north and west to the rich highlands of
Guatemala, but straight north, across the bight of the Pacific
enclosed by this crescent, Guatemala was only twelve hundred
miles away. The male curlew was still hungry, his crop half-
filled, when night began cooling the hot sands of the Parinas
desert. He climbed into the tropic twilight and the female
followed close behind. And he turned north, away from the
low coastland, out into the Pacific where the landfall of
Central America lay twenty-four hours of flying away.

They flew silently, wasting neither breath nor energy
with calling to each other. It would be an ocean crossing
only half as long as the exhausting autumn flight down the
Atlantic from Labrador to South America, but the crowberries of Labrador always assured that the autumn flight could
begin with bodies fat and fully nourished. Now they were
wasted and thin. In two hours their stomachs were gaunt
and empty again.

The southeast trades were left behind after four hours
of flying and they entered the calm, windless area of the
doldrums at the equator. But the sea below was far from
calm. It danced wildly in small, steep waves with foamy,
hissing crests—a battleground of waters where the cold
Humboldt current met the warm flow of the equatorial current and battled for possession of the sea. Then, even by
moonlight, they could see the ocean's color suddenly change
as they left the icy green Humboldt waters behind and flew
on over the deep blue of the equatorial sea. The air became
warmer abruptly.

The moon set and the dawn came. Shortly after dawn
they reached the region of northeast trades, a crosswind

that made flight easier. But the day rapidly turned hot and the stiffling, humid air soon canceled the benefit of the wind.

They flew hour upon hour, the speed of their wingbeats never varying for a moment from the monotonous, grueling three or four beats a second. The glaring sparkle of the sun on the water diminished and finally disappeared as the sun approached its zenith. The sea turned a deeper blue. Then the sun dropped toward the west, the sparkle returned to the wavecrests half a mile below and the air grew hotter still. Since the South American coast had disappeared in the darkness of the night before, there had been nothing to break the flat emptiness of sea except an occasional albatross gliding on gigantic, unmoving wings. But the curlews flew northward unerringly, never deviating, their brains tuned more keenly to the earth's direction-giving forces than any compass could be.

The male, partially breaking air for the female, was suffering greater fatigue. The sharp, periodic pains of his breast muscles had changed to a dull, pressing, unabating ache in which he could feel his heart thumping strenuously. He could have obtained some rest by moving back and letting the female lead, but the realization that she was close behind, drawing on the energy of the air that his strength produced, her flight a dependent part of his own, was a warm and exhilarating thrill that made him cling staunchly to the lead position.

The sun went low in the west and his strength dropped to the point where no amount of stubborn mental drive could keep his wings working at the old harrowing pace. But still he clung to the lead. His wingbeat slackened and the flight speed dropped. As soon as she noticed it, the female, who had been silent for almost twenty-four hours, began a low, throaty, courtship *quirking*, and it gave him strength as no food or rest could do. She repeated it at frequent intervals, and the sun dropped close to the horizon sparkling the sea with a million golden jewels of light, and their wings drove them endlessly on.

The sun was setting when the hard blue of the sea at the horizon ahead of them became edged with a narrow, hazy strip of grey-blue. For several minutes it looked like a cloud, then its texture hardened, and behind it higher in the sky emerged the serrated line of the Guatemalan and Honduran mountain ranges. The outline of the distant volcanic peaks sharpened. The lowland close to the sea changed from blue to green, and a white strip of foaming surf took form at its lower edge. There was still a half hour of daylight when the curlews reached the palm-fringed beach. They commenced eating immediately. When darkness came the pain of hunger and fatigue was already diminishing.

They fed busily all next morning, but the feeding was not good for the beaches were scattered and narrow, and swept clean by the Pacific's surf. By noon the day was very hot, but the curlews flew again. They flew inland now, for this was the Central American summer and the grassy highlands of the interior would have a rich crop of grasshoppers. They flew across the coastal plain which rose gently into the mountains behind. The black fertile volcanic soil was thickly covered with breadfruit trees, coconut palm and plantations of banana trees and sugar cane. In an hour they had climbed a mile above sea level, moving suddenly from tropics to a temperate zone where the air was dry and cool. They climbed higher into mountainous country, then entered a narrow valley which led them through to the rolling tablelands beyond.

They flew four hours and finally landed on a hilly plateau two hundred miles inland from the Pacific. Here, for the first time, the curlews joined the hosts of migrants which were flowing northward to overtake the North American spring. In the forested valleys were swarms of tanagers, thrushes and warblers, all feeding busily to store energy for the long night flights. On the grassy uplands were flocks of other shorebirds and bobolinks. But there was no bird song, for song was the proclamation of the breeding territory, and the breeding territory for most was still two thousand miles away.

On the sloping hills grasshoppers swarmed every- where. The grass was trampled and cropped close by great herds of sheep, so the insects were easy to find. The curlews fed until their crops and stomachs were gorged. With night- fall thousands of other migrants began passing overhead. Except for the occasional one which passed in silhouette across the face of the moon, they were hidden in the dark, but their lisping chorus of flight notes was an uninterrupted signal of their passage. But the curlews waited, for winter still gripped their Arctic nesting grounds and here they could fatten for the final dash north.

They waited a week, feeding well, straggling slowly northward each day. Their bodies grew firm and plump again and with the return of strength the mating urge burned

like a fever within them. By the end of the week they had moved out the Yucatan peninsula to its tip. Five hundred miles northward across the Gulf of Mexico were the swampy shores of Louisiana and Texas, with nothing beyond but the flat unobstructed prairies reaching almost to the Arctic.

... But the greatest killings occurred after the birds had crossed the gulf of Mexico in spring and the great flocks moved northwards up the North American plains.

These flocks reminded prairie settlers of the flights of passenger pigeons and the curlews were given the name of "prairie pigeons." They contained thousands of individuals and would often form dense masses of birds extending half a mile in length and a hundred yards or more in width.

When the flock would alight the birds would cover 40 or 50 acres of ground. During such flights the slaughter was almost unbelievable. Hunters would drive out from Omaha and shoot the birds without mercy until they had literally slaughtered a wagon load of them, the wagons being actually filled, and often with the sideboards on at that. Sometimes when the flight was unusually heavy and the hunters were well supplied with ammunition their wagons were too quickly and easily filled, so whole loads of the birds would be dumped on the prairie, their bodies forming piles as large as a couple of tons of coal, where they would be allowed to rot while the hunters proceeded to refill their wagons with fresh victims.

The compact flocks and tameness of the birds made this slaughter possible, and at each shot usually dozens of the birds would fall. In one specific instance a single shot from an old muzzle-loading shotgun into a flock of these curlews, as they veered by the hunter, brought down 28 birds at once, while for the next half mile every now and then a fatally wounded bird would drop to the ground dead. So dense were the flocks when the birds were turning in their flight that one could scarcely throw a missile into it without striking a bird . . .

In addition to the numerous gunners who shot these birds for local consumption or simply for the love of killing, there developed a class of

professional market hunters, who make it a busi-
ness to follow the flights . . .

The field glass was used by the hunters to
follow their flights . . . There was no difficulty in
getting quite close to the sitting birds, perhaps
within 25 or 35 yards, and when at about this
distance the hunters would wait for them to arise
on their feet, which was the signal for the first
volley of shots. The startled birds would rise and
circle about the field a few times, affording ample
opportunity for further discharge of the guns, and
sometimes would re-alight on the same field, when
the attack would be repeated. Mr. Wheeler has
killed as many as 37 birds with a pump gun at one
rise. Sometimes the bunch would be seen with
the glass alighting in a field two or three miles
away, when the hunters would at once drive to
that field with horse and buggy as rapidly as they
could, relocate the birds, get out, and resume the
fusillade and slaughter . . .

In the eighties the Eskimo curlew began decreasing rapidly . . .

CHAPTER TEN

March had come. In Canada far to the north, robins, blue-
birds and kildeers were already nest-building. Here on the
Yucatan coast the later migrants seethed with the excitement
of the migration time. In winter the overcrowding of the
tropics went unnoticed but when the physiological stirrings
of the breeding cycle started, it drove them outward in a
frantic search for space where each pair could be alone.
Some birds like the swifts and swallows, which could feed
on the wing as they flew, migrated by day, leisurely following
the Mexican coastline north. But most of the birds dammed

up on the Yucatan tip, like a rushing river suddenly blocked, and there they waited, gathering strength, until an evening with favorable wind would send them by thousands into the falling night, out into the wide sweep of the Gulf of Mexico.

One afternoon after two or three days of calm the wind freshened and a restlessness seized the small bird flocks. Bobolinks and thrushes were rising into the air, making short flights out over the water and returning, testing wind and wings. For the curlews, the five-hundred-mile migration across the Gulf would be no more than an average might's flight. But for the smaller songsters, with half the flight speed of the curlews, it was the migration's most rigorous ordeal and the time of starting had to be carefully appraised. By mid-afternoon many of them were not returning from the test flights. They were climbing high above the surf and in twos and threes were continuing seaward until the black specks of their bodies dissolved into the blue of the sky. By sunset the Yucatan shore was strangely quiet. Only the curlews and a few other shorebirds remained.

It was dark and a full moon was rising when the curlews flew. On the other ocean flights the curlews and golden plovers had been alone, but now they flew an oversea flyway that was dotted with other birds. In two hours the curlews began overtaking the smaller birds that had started earlier. The air was filled with call notes, and wings glistened silver in the moonlight all around. There were easier island routes across the Caribbean and Gulf of Mexico along which the birds could have hopped island to island and rarely been out of sight of land. But the land area of the islands was too small to provide food for the migrant hordes, so most of them followed the main land-masses to Yucatan, then crossed the Gulf in a single, non-stop flight. The curlews passed cuckoos that would nest in New England, thrushes and bay-breasted warblers that would mate in the dark spruce forests of the far north, blackpoll warblers that would continue on to Alaska, bobolinks and dickcissels that would fan out across the mid-continental prairies, and brilliant little vermilion flycatchers that would stop and nest as soon as they reached the Louisiana coast. But among the birds that had left Yucatan that afternoon was one species that the curlews never overtook. Many hummingbirds, hardy midgets weighing no more than a tenth of an ounce, had started with the others. But now they were far ahead, outdistancing them all, their tiny wings churning the air with seventy beats a second. Most of the birds would fly twenty hours before they reached the American mainland. The curlews would take ten hours. The hummingbirds would do it in eight.

After four or five hours, the curlews had passed through the flight of smaller birds and were alone again. Suddenly the air grew cool and heavier, giving more lift to their wings, and the easterly trade wind shifted almost to south. Feathery scuds of cloud dimmed the moon at intervals, then the clouds massed into a thick, black, lumpy ceiling and the night was very dark and the gulf waters below were lost in the night's blackness. The wind shifted easterly again, then within fifteen minutes it reversed itself entirely and was blowing from the north. It was a gusty erratic wind. The curlews turned westward to keep it abeam. And then the rain came; it was almost a solid wall of driving water.

1 2 3

After the first explosive outburst, the wind and rain moderated into a steady, lingering storm. It lasted about five hours and the curlews came through the rear of the storm into a clear sky just as the sun was rising. Normally they would have flown on, high over the lagoons and salt marshes of the Texas coast, to land on the prairies of the alluvial plains far inland, but the storm had tired them, their wet wing feathers clung together clammily and responded awkwardly to their pulsing muscles, and the curlews glided low over the beach as soon as they reached the coast.

It was a long, narrow island of sand dunes and grassland that stretched for miles paralleling the coastline. They skimmed across it for a minute or two, seeking a promising spot for feeding before alighting. In the hollows of the sand flats there were numerous ponds with water replenished by the rain of the night before. Hosts of other shorebirds that had left the Yucatan coast ahead of the curlews had also been forced down by the storm and they fed and preened intermittently at the pond edges. The curlews passed over several flocks of plovers and willets, then they breasted a dune and came out suddenly over a broad patchwork of marshy ponds that was dotted with hundreds of Hudsonian curlews. The Hudsonians called to them noisily and the two Eskimo curlews set their wings and pitched down among them.

But they remained with the Hudsonians only that day. At nightfall the two Eskimo curlews flew on alone and in brilliant moonlight two hours later they landed on prairie a hundred miles inland.

Now the migratory restlessness eased again and the curlews were content to wait while the spring moved on ahead of them. Instinct, not reasoning, told them that all the obstacles of the migration were behind and now for three thousand miles to the Arctic there were only the great flatlands of the American and Canadian plains, teeming with food, lacking mountains, lacking even a range of hills large enough to interfere with the home-coming flight. It was the home stretch and they could span it in a week if need be.

But the migratory urge was temporarily dead. The curlews didn't know that the tundra would not be ready for the nesting for more than two months yet. They only knew that the Texas prairies were rich with the insect life of awakening spring. And they felt an urge to stay.

They waited three weeks, moving barely another hundred miles inland in the whole period. Flocks of the smaller migrants streamed past them overhead almost every night, for they would nest far below the Arctic in breeding grounds that were already greening with spring. When the time came, the curlews would span in one night what the small birds covered in three.

It was early April when the restlessness seized them and they began making brief night flights again. They flew easily, stopping always many hours before dawn, sometimes not moving at all for several days at a time. They would wait as the spring moved northward far ahead of them, then in

a couple of rapid night flights they would overtake and pass the spring again and wait for it to catch up. The signal to move was the blooming of the willows on the river bottomlands. When the fluffy catkins opened, dusting the evening breezes with the yellow pollen, they would take to the air and fly until they reached a point farther north where the willow buds were unopened and the prairie grass still brown. Then they would wait, feeding luxuriantly on the capsules of grasshopper eggs which their sensitive bills could feel in the damp soil, and when the willow catkins pierced their buds the curlews would fly northward again.

Each week they moved faster, for the advancing spring picked up speed as it reached more northern latitudes.

THE AUK
A Quarterly Journal of Ornithology
Published by
The American Ornithologists' Union
Lancaster, Pa.

General notes. Natural hybrids between Dendroica coronata and D. auduboni . . . Rivoli's hummingbird (Eugenes fulgens) in Colorada . . . Eskimo

curlew in Texas. Two Eskimo curlews which appeared to be a mated pair were seen in March at
Galveston, Texas, by the writer and a number of
Houston observers. The birds were amongst a huge
assemblage of marsh and shorebirds, including
buff-breasted and other sandpipers, black-bellied
plovers, eastern and western willets, various her-
ons, and hundreds of Hudsonian curlews. All
were feeding over a wide area of sand flats, shallow ponds and grassy patches on Galveston Island,
which parallels the coast. Nearness of the Eskimo
curlews to Hudsonians gave fine opportunity for
comparison. Smaller size of the Eskimo and shorter
length of bill were obvious, and movements of the
birds, in brilliant mid-afternoon sunlight, clearly
showed the large black wing area and lack of me-
dian head stripe. Fully an hour was spent checking
every identification mark through eight-power
glasses at a range of less than one hundred yards
from our parked car . . . as is often the case along
the Texas gulf coast during spring migration, a
heavy rainstorm and change of wind from south
to north during the previous night brought down
a swarming visitation of migrants.—(Sgt.) Joseph M.
Heiser, Jr. . . .

A summary of the spring migration. Undoubtedly
the most noteworthy record was the observation
of a pair of Eskimo curlews on Galveston Island,

Texas, the first acceptable record of this species in several years. For twenty years only an occasional lone Eskimo curlew has been seen and the fact that these were probably a mated pair makes it a record of great significance. As long as one pair remains there is hope that the species may yet escape extinction . . .

CHAPTER ELEVEN

Now it was corn-planting time on the Nebraska and Dakota prairies and great steel monsters that roared like the ocean surf were crossing and recrossing the stubble fields leaving black furrows of fresh-turned soil in orderly ranks behind them. Most of the shorebirds shunned the growling machines and the men who were always riding them. Yellowlegs and sandpipers would stop their feeding and watch warily when the plowman was still hundreds of yards off, then if the great machine came closer they would take wing, whistling shrilly, and not alight again until they were a mile

away. But the Eskimo curlews had little fear. Far back in the species' evolutionary history they had learned that, for them, a highly developed fear was unnecessary. Their wings were strong and their flight so rapid that they could ignore danger until the last moment, escaping fox or hawk easily in a last-second flight. So their fear sense had disappeared, as all unused faculties must, and while other shorebirds relied on wariness and timidity for survival, the Eskimo curlew relied entirely on its strength of wing.

The curlews followed the roaring machines closely, for the white grubs and cutworms that the plows turned up were a rich and abundant food.

All the time their reproductive glands had been swelling in the annual springtime rhythm of development, the development keeping pace with the northward march of spring, so that their bodies and the tundra would become ready simultaneously for the nesting and egg-laying. As the physical development came close to the zenith of its cycle, there was an intensification of emotional development too. With high body temperatures and rapid metabolism, every process of living is faster and more intense in birds than any other creature. When the breeding time approaches they court and love with a fervor and passion that matches the intensity of all their other life processes.

Now many times a day the male curlew's mounting emotion boiled over into a frantic display of love. It had become a much more violent display than the earlier acts of courtship. First the male would spring suddenly into the air and hover on quivering wings while he sang the clear, rolling, mating song—a song much more liquid and mellow now than at any other time of year. After a few seconds his wings would beat violently and he would rise almost straight upward, his long legs trailing behind, until he was a couple of hundred feet above the prairie. There he would hover again, singing louder so that bursts of the song would reach the female, bobbing and whistling excitedly far below. Then

he would close his wings and dive straight toward her, swerving upward again in the last few feet above her head and landing several yards away.

Panting with emotion, singing in loud bursts, his throat and breast inflated with air and the feathers thrust outward, he would hold his wings extended gracefully over his back until the female invited the climactic approach. She would bob quickly with quivering wings and call with the harsh, food-begging notes of a fledgling bird. Then he would dash toward her, his wings beating vigorously again so that he was almost walking on air. Their swollen breasts would touch. The male's neck would reach past her own and he would tenderly preen her brown wing feathers with his long bill.

It would last only a few seconds, and the male would dash away again. He would pick up the largest grub he could find and return quickly to the female. Then he would place it gently into her bill. She would swallow it, her throat feathers would suddenly flatten, her wings stop quivering, and the love-making abruptly end. For as yet the courtship feeding was the love climax; their bodies were not yet ready for the final act of the mating.

For a couple of hours after each courtship demonstration the passion and tenseness of the approaching mating time would relax, for the love display was a stopgap that satisfied them emotionally while they awaited the time for the physical consummation.

They moved north steadily, a couple of hundred miles each night. The male's sexual development matured first and he was ready for the finalizing of the mating. His passion became a fierce, unconstrainable frenzy and he spent most of each day in violent display before the female. But with each courtship feeding her tenseness suddenly relaxed and the display would end.

It was mid-May and the newly-plowed sections of rolling, Canadian prairie steamed in the warming sun. They followed closely behind the big machine with the roar like an ocean surf. The grubs were fat and they twisted convulsively in the few seconds that the sun hit them before the curlews snapped them up. Now the snows of the tundra would be melting. In the ovaries of the female the first of her four developing eggs was ready for the life-giving fertilization.

The male flung himself into the air, his love song wild and vibrant. He hovered high above the black soil of the prairie with its fresh striated pattern of furrows The roar of the big machine stopped and the curlew hardly noted the change, for his senses were focused on the female quivering excitedly against the dark earth far below. The man on the tractor sat stiffly, his head thrown back, staring upward, his eyes shaded against the sun with one hand. The curlew dove earthward and the female called him stridently. He plucked a grub from the ground and dashed at her, his neck outstretched, wings fluttering vigorously. He saw the man leap down from the tractor seat and run toward a fence where his jacket hung. Normally, at this, even the curlews would have taken wing in alarm, but now the female accepted the courtship feeding and her wings still quivered in a paroxysm of mating passion. She crouched submissively

for the copulation and in the ecstasy of the mating they were blind to everything around them.

The thunder burst upon them out of a clear and vivid sky. The roar of it seemed to come from all directions at once. The soil around them was tossed upward in a score of tiny black splashes like water being pelted with hail.

The male flung himself into the air. He flew swiftly, clinging close to the ground so that no speed was lost in climbing
for height. Then he saw the female wasn't with him. He
circled back, *keering* out to her in alarm. Her brown body
still crouched on the field where they had been. The male
flew down and hovered a few feet above her, calling wildly.

Then the thunder burst a second time and a violent
but invisible blow blasted two of the biggest feathers from
one of his extended wings. The impact twisted him completely over in mid-air and he thudded into the earth at the
female's side. Terrified and bewildered at a foe that could
strike without visible form, he took wing again. Then the
bewilderment overcame his terror and he circled back to
his mate a second time. Now she was standing, *keering* also
in wild panic. Her wings beat futilely several times before
she could raise herself slowly into the air. She gained height
and flight speed laboriously and the male moved in until he
was close beside her.

He continued to call clamorously as he flew, but the female became silent. They flew several minutes and the field with the terrifying sunlight thunder was left far behind. But the female flew slowly. She kept dropping behind and the male would circle back and urge her on with frantic pleas, then he would outdistance her again.

Her flight became slower and clumsy. One wing was

beating awkwardly and it kept throwing her off balance. The soft buffy feathers of the breast under the wing were turning black and wet. She started calling to him again, not the loud calls of alarm but the soft, throaty *quirking* of the love display.

Then she dropped suddenly. Her wings kept fluttering weakly, it was similar to the excited quivering of the mating moment, and her body twisted over and over until it embedded itself in the damp earth below.

The male called wildly for her to follow. The terror of the ground had not yet left him. But the female didn't move. He circled and re-circled above and his plaintive cries must have reached her, but she didn't call back.

A long time later he overcame the fear and landed on the ground close to her. He preened her wing feathers softly with his bill. When the night came the lure of the tundra became a stubborn, compelling call, for the time of the nesting was almost upon them. He flew repeatedly, whistling back to her, then returning, but the female wouldn't fly with him. Finally he slept close beside her.

At dawn he hovered high in the grey sky, his lungs swelling with the cadence of his mating song. Now she didn't respond to the offer of courtship feeding. The tundra call was irresistible. He flew again and called once more. Then he leveled off, the rising sun glinted pinkly on his feathers, and he headed north in silence, alone.

The snow-water ponds and the cobblestone bar and the dwarfed willows that stood beside the S-twist of the tundra river were unchanged. The curlew was tired from

the long flight. But when a golden plover flew close to the territory's boundary he darted madly to the attack. The Arctic summer would be short. The territory must be held in readiness for the female his instinct told him soon would come.